CW01011579

Copyright © 1996 Scott Adlerberg
Cover Design © 1996 Press-Tige Publishing

All rights reserved, including the right to reproduce this book
or portions therein in any form whatsoever.

For information address:
        Press-Tige Publishing
        291 Main Street
        Catskill, New York 12414

First Press-Tige Edition 1996

Printed in the United States of America

ISBN 1-57532-068-1

SPIDERS AND FLIES

by

Scott Adlerberg

PROLOGUE

In the evening, when I have nothing else to do, I sometimes walk to the seafront shack where the men bet on the fighting cocks. Although I make no wagers, I enjoy the action, the turmoil centered on the flapping wings and the cropped feathers. There with the noisy crowd I watch the battles, and I never flinch as the blood drips, the spurs slash, the vicious red heads peck at each other. But the sound of the shirt-sleeved men yelling their guttural creole grates on my ears; the cigarette smoke curling off the ends of a hundred stubs assaults my nostrils; soon I begin to feel nauseous breathing the odor of perspiration forming under fleshy arms. I withdraw. I stroll over to the Abricotier and sit at an outside table, the better to smell the water, to hear it licking at the hulls of the boats tied to the wharf.

Anchored yachts rock in the bay and the starlit view across the surf reassures me; sailing vessels, more than planes, hold the promise of escape. I tell myself that anytime now I will be able to leave this island, I will have somewhere to go. The waitress comes, a sullen woman in a calf-length frock, and I order a ti-punch. She drags her slippered feet inside and when she shuffles back from the bar she lifts everything off a platter -- the glass and the bottle, the slice of lime, a tiny spoon, a silver dish containing brown sugar. And I combine the ingredients myself, that's the custom, pouring the rum in last. Throughout the tropics people favor the rum made in their own locale, but here the claims of producing the best have merit. I could never again drink the Puerto Rican stuff I used to buy at home. My taste has changed. But a lot has changed since I had to run; in exile I have learned to adapt. Foreigner that I am, I have held on, I have managed, though I realize I could be stuck in a less-enticing place than Martinique.

If you have to lie low, if the threat of prison obliges you to live abroad, then why not do it where the sun shines hot and the sky at dusk turns into a gorgeous blue flame? Who can tell? Lisa and I might have spent our honeymoon in the Caribbean. As it is, I am here alone.

Chapter One

Some time ago there came to the residence where I stay a group of American college students. The six of them five boys and a girl, had failed French at their Louisiana school, and to make up the course, they had accepted the opportunity to visit Martinique and learn about the culture. During their month stay they had a busy schedule, and for awhile I had little trouble avoiding them. Still, they occupied rooms in the same corridor as mine, and that forced me on occasion to pass them. I would nod hello and keep walking.

"Wait," the girl said once. "You're from New York?"

I stopped and answered. It seemed that somebody else living in the dorm had told her that.

"What are you doing here?" she asked. "In Martinique, I mean."

One night shortly after this they all gathered in her room and I could hear them singing. Zouk and reggae held no appeal; after two weeks in the Caribbean world they sang American songs with relish and nostalgia.

'Oh give me the people to free my soul
 I want to get lost in your rock and roll
 And drift awayyyy'

They faded into silence, a brief silence, and I heard a maudlin cry:

"I want to go home, goddammit!"

But I thought, you don't know what it is to miss home. Not really. You can't possibly know unless you're without a home to return to. I'm like that. I'm the one who's drifting.

In the dark, from my mattress, I stared at the shadow of a roach sliding along the line of books on my shelf. Down the hall they carried on, and the very thing I feared happened. When I got up and headed for the bathroom, tiptoeing on the olive-green carpet, the door opened and a head popped out, a face pink and flaky with sunburn.

"You need to use more of that lotion," I said.

"Not all of us have a natural tan."

"Ha-ha-ha."

"Only kidding. Want some rum and Coke?"

His moist hand took my arm and urged me forward to join them.

"You gotta get drunk with us once, Paul."

I sat in the wooden chair he offered and thanked him for the drink, served in a white coffee mug. He had made it strong, but the soda was warm.

"People here don't usually have this mix," I said.

"They don't?"

"The rum's so good there's no reason to hide the flavor."

The students, holding their cups, had settled themselves on the two beds. I examined their faces, young and jovial, and I could not believe that just a year earlier I had been in school myself. At 24, after what I had done, after what I had been compelled to do, I felt like an old man with nothing but rotten memories left.

"Yes," I said in reply to a question. "I've been on the island for months."

"How could you take it for that long?"

"It's not too bad."

"In Fort de France the whole time?"

"The whole time," I said. "Mostly in this residence."

"Not the best of accommodations."

"That's why it's cheap. Cheap by Martinican standards."

"And the showers..."

"They wake you up in the morning," I said.

"They're freezing."

I admitted that I missed the baseball season and that although I could follow movies in French, I hated watching English-language films that are dubbed.

"So?" The girl, my questioner, smiled, and she could not have had cheeks more rosy with innocence. "We came because it was this or summer school. But you...nothing keeps you here. Why don't you go back to New York?"

"I can't."

"What's stopping you? Don't you have family there?"

I shut my eyes and drank the rest of the rum and Coke. For a moment it lightened the load I had in my brain.

"I killed someone," I said, looking straight at the girl. "If I go back, I'll be arrested."

These were considered humorous statements, and while they laughed, I departed, saying (and this was also true) that I had to give an English lesson early in the morning.

"Life here costs. Without a lot of money it can be tough."

I had difficulty getting to sleep and when I did, I dreamt of the house I had destroyed.

Chapter Two

Lisa had a grey cat, a green-eyed creature that she adored, and I can recall the night, here in Martinique, when I awoke unable to breathe and saw her pet sitting on my chest. I kicked off the sheet and rolled around, intent on gripping the furry throat. My hands bumped together, locked, squeezed and finally I separated them. I massaged my forehead, thinking, and as my terror subsided, I scolded myself. I knew that no animal, not even hers, could come back to life and materialize in the tropics to haunt me. The cat had died in the fire that obliterated the ancestral mansion of its owner, and what I had seen crouched on my chest was the last faint image from a nightmare. Sticky with sweat, too shaken to sleep, I rose in my underpants and tramped down the hall to the shower. The frigid water felt good for a change and after I had wiped myself off, I decided to go out. My room, in need of dusting, seemed oppressive.

It was a Friday. I put on rakish clothes and walked along the canal, passing the food trucks and the crepe stands, moving among the people who had collected on the strip. The facades of the buildings provided gaudy illumination, the glitter of neon, and on the arching bridge, against the yellow railings, lovers inspired by the dazzle kissed. Gaping mouths took in the flow of bottled beer; cheese-smudged palms held pizza slices on aluminum foil. I watched a pack of motorcycle riders weave by, dodging a wheel, smelling burnt rubber, and at the disco, the Elysee Matignon, I handed my francs to the man guarding the door. Most of the time I shun night clubs, but when I am in a specific mood, I enjoy mingling with the trendy set. In the Elysee Matignon your admission tag entitled you to a free drink. I went directly to the bar asking for a Planter's Punch. I liked its fruity taste, but I knew at once that I had erred. I knew because I always come to a disco smashed. The liquor helps me loosen up and lets me tolerate the pounding music. But tonight I had broken with habit, had arrived sober, and in the Martinican clubs the price of drinks after that first one is exorbitant. Limited to the single cocktail, I remained clearheaded, a state inappropriate for dancing. And now, as I finished my Planter's, as I plucked the cherry off the swizzle stick, I began to think again of Lisa's cat, the grey Persian, and that thought led to a mental picture of Lisa, the girl I had married.

Out among the dancers, among the swinging hips and the undulant elbows, I tried to get my mind off Lisa. I tried to lose myself in the music, a monotonous pulse, and over bobbing heads, in the kaleidoscopic light, I scanned the room, observed the girls. Were any of them alone? So it appeared, but those without male companions had their attention focused on themselves. Along the walls were mirrors, ceiling-height sheets of glass that reflected back the elegance of the chandeliers, the stone tables, the plush blue sofas where resting couples lounged arm in arm, head to shoulder, eyes staring at the people in sensuous motion. And into the mirrors these women gazed, admiring themselves as they danced on the edges of the checker-tiled floor. To be fair about it, I cannot say it was only women who pressed themselves close to the mirrors; men did, too. But since my interest was heterosexual, the ones who annoyed me with their evident self-enchantment were the females. In black mini-skirts and sharp heels, in dresses that hugged their breasts and shimmied up their thighs, in red pants glued to the skin, with hair thick and long or in Nefertitti braids, every coiffure perfectly designed, perfectly groomed, with features that had been shaped by years of mixing with the French, their complexions African-black, honey-brown, a touch darker than white, thus the Martinican women before me lived up to their reputation for being the most attractive and stylish women in the Caribbean.

They have what some visitors call an aristocratic quality - I prefer to call it arrogance - and a man who speaks uncertain French, as I do, can have his problems trying to relate to them. Let me give you an example.

While out at the beach one afternoon, I suddenly remembered that I had to contact one of my English students. I found the nearest public phone and along with a few other guys, I waited for a woman to end her conversation. It went on and on; five minutes stretched into fifteen. Everybody else looked impassive, but I started to curse under my breath. Could you imagine someone in New York City doing what she did? The people standing by would raise hell. So I approached this girl, this handsome girl in a pink off-the-shoulder blouse, and in my careful French, I asked her to get off the phone. Despite my courteous smile, I received a disdainful glance and she continued talking without having missed a beat. I stamped my foot; I whistled a song to nag her; even if I had seen another phone in the area, I would have refused to use it. My impatience had grown into anger now, and after more waiting, I exploded. I screamed at the girl, insulting her both in French and English. But nobody said anything to support me (the Martinicans can be too genteel, too reserved) and the girl simply turned away, tossed her head as if harassed by a mosquito. That did it. I grabbed her single braid, a tightly twisted ponytail, and without a warning I pulled on it hard. As her neck snapped back, the girl hollered; the telephone slipped from her hand and fell toward the sidewalk. Through the earpiece I heard a man's voice, stunned, begging her for a response, and I released her then, only to find that the others were shouting at me, their words incomprehensible. Had I misjudged them? I had thought they would applaud my action. Outnumbered, I saw no purpose in arguing and before anyone could get violent, I took off.

But later, as I recalled the incident in my room, I realized that something about the girl had disturbed me from the first. Her ponytail, the snakish length of black hair, had reminded me of Lisa. On our wedding day Lisa had arranged her hair in a similar fashion, and Lisa was the one, Lisa and her family, who had ruined my life. That clan manipulated me so much I came to see my life with them as a nightmare, and I think I can be excused for what I did to get away from them. I felt that I had to kill Lisa to save myself. Yes, I lived through a nightmare with that family and everything I do is shadowed by what I remember of them.

In any event, what I'm trying to say is that I know I overreacted with the Martinican girl. I didn't have to pull her hair. But I used to be different. I used to be happy; Lisa and her family made me what I've become. What they did to me I can never forgive, and I think my original point, the thing I was saying about the Martinican women, still holds. You can understand why I called them arrogant.

Since coming to the island I have had no success with them, and at the disco that Friday, my frustration caused me physical pain. I loathed the throbbing music to which they moved. I could take no more of watching the ones slithering in front of the mirrors, dancing a love dance to themselves. Surrounded by bodies, I felt stifled and with a fist held out, I pushed my way to the steps leading down to the exit.

I crossed the street and leaned against the canal wall, arms dangling over the top. The water below was oily and sluggish. It had a black-green color in the striated light of the lamps built along the embankments. Here every day, before sunset, the painted dories come in from the sea; the fishermen unload their catches by the big, covered market. And in the air's odor I could taste fish; I inhaled the scents of melted butter and chocolate crepes; the smoke in the street alerted my tongue to the lamb being cooked on charcoal grilles. Behind me on the pavement a portable generator whirred, powering one of the snack vans, and the gangly *enfants* on their motorcycles could not resist revving their engines as they cruised up and down the strip. Weekend nights by the canal last well into the dawn and the presence of the liveliness around me, the banter, the flirtations, the carousing, increased my depression.

I plodded off, a somnabulist among the animated. My eyes caught glimpses of mouths against mouths, of hands intertwined. A bottle shattered, somebody giggled, and a girl to my left smelled like orange blossoms. Inside my chest I carried a fire, the fire of contained rage, and I turned a corner as fast as I could, seeking the refuge of empty streets. But where could I go? My room meant isolation and the disquiet of insomnia, and what good would it do me to sit in a bar, to fill myself with alcohol?

Perhaps I could find Charles; perhaps he was on his boat for the night and had it moored, as he often does, to the landing pier at the Abricotier. When desperate, when at my lowest, I am diverted by his video collection and the privacy of his 17-footer allows me to relax as we watch.

Smut on the water you could name his aquatic cinema, and of course every film obeys the standard premises, adheres to formula. You see the splayed legs and the wagging rumps, the tangled hedonists and the blissful turbulence of their orgasms, the women moaning, "Yes, yes, yes," or "oui, oui, oui." And Charles, a connoisseur, trembles with agitation, commenting on the movies throughout. "Look what she's doing...can you believe how well she does it?...what a talent she has...what a blonde....isn't she a fantastic blonde?" Yes, I thought, I could drop in on Charles. I could go there expecting amusement, but I knew that after an hour or so I would become bored. The repetition of the scenes would wear me down. Charles and his talk would get on my nerves, and I would leave that boat feeling a sense of hollow relief. Charles, bilingual, is my one genuine friend in Martinique, but I can only stand so much of his company.

In the center of town the bells tolled twice. And near the cathedral were the prostitutes, five or six familiar women clustered around an intersection. Opposite the church I paused, regarding the tall spire, and I fingered the cash in my trouser pocket. I had never spent a franc on these professionals, and they still struck me as repulsive. They were rawboned and dull-eyed, camouflaged by garish cosmetics. I said to myself, 'don't waste your money.'

Left foot, right foot, left foot; I kept on walking the tranquil streets and my path was as aimless as my thoughts.

Chapter Three

About once a month I receive a letter from Larry. He has managed to hold his apartment in the Bronx, but he often expresses a wish, contingent upon his finances, to get out of New York and join me in exile. In Larry's opinion, I am living 'the' life and any fugitive in hiding would gladly switch positions with me. I achieved my objectives, he maintains; I disentagled myself from Lisa, got clear of her menacing relatives, and evaded capture by the police. How can I brood? I am, he says, in a tropical paradise and as if inclined to convince me of the fact, he waxes rhapsodic over the postcards that I send him. Through these pictures, as an armchair traveler, he imagines himself lying flat on the palm-shaded beaches; he envisions himself climbing the misty slopes of the dead volcano.

Week after week I mail him the ready-made photographs, the snapshots of luxuriant mountains, purple hibiscus, silver cascades, emerald pools in the rain forest. I make him pine for the greenness of the island, the lushness of the flora, and I tempt him further with a card that shows a village harbor glistening bronze under a crimson evening sky. Let him dream, I think. Let him fantasize about the Caribbean. In the Bronx he meets enough gutter rats, so I feel no need to dwell on the vermin that forage through the rubbish piles here. Why should I bring up the danger posed by the scrawny dogs, by the overabundance of scavenging strays that roam through Fort de France and keep me awake nights with their barking? I would shoot them all if I had a gun and I would love to eliminate the water bugs, the large black beetles that have opened a tunnel between the canal and my room. They come out of nowhere, scurrying across the floor, legs tapping on the wood, and their protective shells are so hard that I have to strike once, twice, three goddamned times with the sole of my sneaker. And when at last I have crushed one, as I am flinging it out my window with a spoon, I notice a swarm of ants tearing into the bread crumb left upon my table. The war against the insects, unappeasable invaders, goes on and on and on.

Oh, I guess I could mention these things to Larry. I should, in fact, so that he can form a truer idea of Martinique. But he wants letters that highlight glamor, the tropics of sun, sea and sex, and like a compromising author, I yield to my reader's demands, though I have to use my imagination when describing my alleged romantic adventures.

*****

At the time I was planning the murder, I unfolded a map of the world and thought about where I would go to elude pursuit. I chose the Caribbean because of the climate and despite a sparse knowledge of French, studied for a year in high school, I zeroed in on the French Antilles. Heads for Martinique, tails for Guadeloupe; and the coin came up heads. I looked forward to a hybrid island; grillework balconies in town, sugar cane fields in the country. Breakfasts would consist of passion fruit juice served with croissants; I would eat duck *orange* in a restaurant smelling of red jasmine. There would be rum and the wine delivered from Bordeaux, there would be mangos and bananas as well as French pastries, and I thought of drumming music and Mardi Gras and magnificent villas that had been erected by people in chains. Martinique seemed exotic from a distance and my decision to go there almost consoled me for the act I was about to commit.

I arrived. I went to a bank and put in my money. But it dwindled quickly, and from a cottage resort for tourists, I moved to the inexpensive residence. Home is the cramped room with the sagging mattress and anybody eager to see me, or to slip me a message, need only walk to the brown door at the end of the hall. Number thirteen it says; how appropriate. And to help myself feel attached to the room, I have taped to the door a piece of paper with my name, Paul Raven, written across it.

It's strange. The luxuries of the recent past, the appliances I took for granted, seem like comforts I never had, just dreamt. In this monk's cell I have no refrigerator and I prepare my food - pasta, lentils, rice, beans - on a camping stove fitted with a butane cannister. Living in a dump like this you learn to tolerate the insufficient privacy; you ignore the loud conversations, the booming radios and the noises, after dark, from certain beds. You become accustomed to the bathroom sinks getting clogged, murky water trapped in the basins, and inside the shower stalls you develop a particular skill with your fingers; by its very edge you can lift up and flip toward the drain the hair-

Scott Adlerberg

streaked keg of soap that the previous person in the shower forgot. I keep myself supplied with toilet paper, since the residence furnishes none, and if I have no choice but to use one of the seatless bowls, I squat above it without allowing my buttocks to touch the stained enamel. It smells of urine and feces and mildew in there, and whenever I go in late at night, I hear the resident cat digging through the lavatory trash pail, searching in the refuse for edible scraps dropped in that day by the lodgers. I pull the cord, the toilet sucks down the water, and as I slide back the latch and open the door, the plastic bag in the can rustles and out springs the cat, skidding across the blue floor, white tail vanishing around a corner.

The place has 25 rooms along two hallways, but nobody in it, not the university students or the passing travelers or the veterans like me, has the slightest concern for its condition. We are indifferent and so is the woman who runs everything for the management. She shows up sporadically, distributes the mail that has gathered dust in our post office box. Then she asks us whether the two Haitian maids have been coming each morning and doing their work. "Absolument," we reply, no matter how filthy the residence looks. "Chaque matin. Comme toi." She grits her teeth, spins on her high heels and carries her girth into the bureau. Some of us hear our names shouted; hands rifle through wallets for the rent money. After she departs, we the lodgers have to watch the entrance again, and whoever among us leaves the premises locks the gate behind himself. "Les clochards," a girl says - the tramps. We don't want them sauntering in because whenever they do, they sleep on the balcony. We have enough pests to cope with as it is.

I laugh at her quip, but when I return to my room I slap the wall in exasperation. With Lisa I lived in a mansion and had I stuck with our marriage, I would have had a real home. As a child I had done my playing on the streets of New York City, but after the loss of my parents, shot one night when they were mugged by a gang, I joined her in the house that stood all alone in the Hudson Valley. When had we met? I cannot recall. I only know that we had been close a long time. Every year she had visited us in Manhattan or I had gone to her family's country estate. It seemed logical that with my parents dead, hers would take me in. I had no blood relations left and my best friend in New York, Larry, was recovering from the accident that had mangled his face.

14

Larry's father, preoccupied with his son's convalescence, had no intention of adopting me. So I waved farewell to the skyscrapers, I got into a car with Lisa and her mother, and up at their house they gave me a room, connected to Lisa's by a double door.

"Whatever we have is for you also," they assured me, and I felt at ease. I had lost my parents but there were compensations, and what I especially could not get over was my new bed. In the city I had slept on a mattress the width of a crib; this one was fluffy and wide, a four-poster antique. Lisa had a bed just like it and from night to night, wearing our pajamas, we shuttled through the connecting door. Each of us was twelve years old and we began our sexual bouts with comical games, tentative probings. And her parents approved, for they must have known. Given free reign, we continued and as we made our discoveries, as our pleasures increased, I admitted to myself that this misfortune, this terrible loss, had actually resulted in good fortune.

I loved the country. I settled into rustic life as though born to it. Lisa taught me horseback riding, and once I had mastered the techniques of the saddle, I explored the region with her as my guide. We poked into caves, rode through the wooded hills. During the summer we plunged into ponds and cold brooks, during the winter we skied on trails winding through the snow-flecked pines, and in the autumn, when the apples ripened, we picked the green and red fruits and assisted in the family's cider production. The fermented cider from the Hudson basin was the first alcoholic drink I ever had, and even here in Martinique, with its variety of excellent liquors, I miss that cider. I miss the potent froth and the delicious, stinging taste.

I did indeed have a home in Lisa's ancestral house, and no existence could have been more idyllic. When high school ended, we went to the same college and after that we decided on marriage. Neither of her parents objected; the prospect pleased them. We set the date and began making the arrangements. But then, a week before the wedding, the nightmare started. Lisa acquainted me with her secret relatives. She took me to see the entire monstrous clan, and she told me what I, as her husband, would have to do for them.

Was it a dream? Am I dreaming now as I remember it? I wish it had never happened, but I know it did, and I know that Lisa's revelation about 'my duties' is what led to the murder.

15

Chapter Four

I was approaching consciousness that morning and something shaggy brushed my cheek. Something damp grazed my mouth. I awoke with a cry and a shudder and together these must have startled the cat, prompting it to step on my right arm. It scratched me below the wrist; I cursed as I felt the oozing blood. The grey Persian had already jumped off the bed and I heard it scrambling across the carpet. 'Why don't you go to hell?' I whispered, and glared at the creature as it leapt up onto its favorite post, the windowsill on the far side of the room. It backed against the gauzy drapes and I watched it clean itself, lick itself all over as if it thought its contact with me had left it contaminated. Satisfied with its washing, the cat reclined on the perch, legs tucked beneath its belly, and in the sparkle of its green eyes, riveted to my face, I could have sworn I discerned a human intelligence, a hint of gloating ridicule.

"Dammit. This thing is demonic."

The disturbance had awakened Lisa and she hoisted herself up, shifted over on the bed and came down with her chin and one of her hands propped upon my stomach. My hard muscles supported the weight without any strain; two of her fingers pinched my navel. Lisa grinned at me with the childlike softness of a person half asleep, but her body went rigid the moment she noticed my wound, the blood streaming along my arm. Her drowsiness gone, she turned her head and looked at the cat. The diaphanous curtains behind the animal refracted the sunlight, and the oblique shafts illuminated parts of Lisa -- her angular cheekbones, her sinewy neck, the broad shoulders in the striped pajama shirt. I saw her lips shrivel into a mock-serious frown.

"Did he cut you again? Mean cat."

Lisa changed her position so that her legs were straddling mine. Through my drawers I could feel her silk panties. Bending forward, she kissed me on the mouth and as she did her black hair covered my face. Beneath her like that I felt snug, and I caressed her tongue with my own. The cat meowed. Lisa laughed into my throat and raised her head. Tender as a nurse, she grasped my bleeding arm, and while I waited, knowing what was to come, she lifted my arm up for inspection. She had one hand on my elbow and one near my injured wrist, and blood and more blood kept dribbling onto the white linen.

"Does it hurt?" she asked.

"Not badly," I answered. "Not any worse than usual."

I had scars here and there; the cat bore me a definite malice. But every time it slashed my flesh (not once had it clawed anybody else) Lisa would do what she did now. She fastened her lips to my cut and began to drain the opening. As always, I enjoyed her oral remedy, the voluptuousness of having her drink my blood, and in my growing excitement, I pushed my waist upwards. I smelled the balsam scent in her hair. Lisa rocked as she lapped at the wound and I started to loosen her pajama shirt, undoing each button slowly.

"One second."

She had stopped sucking. A patch of scarlet was smeared across her dimpled chin. The cat squealed, a jarring noise, and I nestled deeper into my quilted pillow. While staring at me, Lisa swung herself to my side and with her left hand she reached into my drawers. I felt myself gripped, felt the warmth of her rubbing palm. Lisa climbed back on top of me, naked, and the hold of her knees against my pelvis became a firm vise. Though she had staunched the bleeding, she put her mouth to my wrist again and I grabbed a clump of her satiny hair, pressing it to my nose for another whiff of the herbal fragrance. Above me Lisa quivered and swayed, but I could not relax completely because of the damned cat. It kept whining, a resentful voyeur.

"The bastard is jealous of me," I said. "How do you shut him up?"

Lisa let go of my arm and made a piping sound. A glance toward the window told me that she had communicated, for the Persian had disappeared from the sill. Its rapid padding steps crossed the carpet, and I saw the ridge of the curved back enter Lisa's room, where the cat liked to lie by the radiator.

"Thanks," I said.

At the door there was knocking and we heard the respectful voice of Wilson, the manservant. "You two awake?" he said. "Breakfast will be ready in about ten minutes."

"Be right there," Lisa said.

"Very good."

His soft-soled shoes receded down the hall. Lisa and I both

17

smiled. I wrenched her forward by tugging on her hair. She began to pummel my shoulders with her fists, and at the conclusion we went into a tight embrace.

"One week," Lisa said after we had pulled apart. "One long week."

"It's only a piece of paper," I said. "It shouldn't change anything."

"True, but you'll be an official member of the family."

"I thought I am."

"Not quite," she said. "But after the marriage, yes. After the ceremony. There'll be a big party and everyone will come to that."

"Everyone?"

"All the relatives."

"What relatives?"

"You'll meet them today," Lisa said. "Today's the day."

After the meal we saddled up and took the horses out of the stable. We led them over a gravel path that cut a line to the woods in the west. I held my reins loosely and as I bounced in time to the loping of my auburn colt, I kept my eyes on Lisa's hair, weaved into a braid for riding convenience. She had chosen a stallion, all rippling muscle under a tawny hide, and the energetic creature was gaining speed, opening a gap between us. Lisa let out a whoop of joy. The long black braid jiggled and danced just as the horse's tail did. In cowboy boots, unwrinkled dungarees, and a close-fitting grey sweater, Lisa personified equestrian elegance. I admired her posture sitting in the pommeled seat, the way she could keep her back arched and her jaw up, the way her legs with their slight bend looked molded to the stallion's flanks. Again she whooped, head tilted toward the sky, and when her elbows flapped outward, I knew she had used her reins to whip the horse, bidding it to run faster. I followed her example and in a moment we were galloping. The hooves beating against the pebbles created sparks; I listened to my colt snorting, clearing its nostrils as it warmed to the rapid pace. No clouds shown in the silvery blue above us and the gusts of autumnal wind were biting. Chilled, I turned up the collar on my suede jacket.

Across the lawn to our left stood the impressive house, porticoed mansion, and as we thundered by it a white wisp of curtain moved. The sun's reflection shimmered off a sliding pane of glass. Lisa's parents had opened the picture window in

18

their bedroom, and with an easy lolling gait, the two of them advanced onto their terrace. From that level, three floors up, they regarded us, she in a billowy robe, he in a lavender dressing gown, and while they loitered at the railing, Lisa caught my attention by raising her hand and making a fist. Her parents responded in kind, their arms swinging. I don't know why exactly, but seeing those gestures congealed my blood. A painful tremor shot through my system. They all had signaled one another and their pale fists lifted high conveyed a sinister meaning. Somehow I knew that they had exchanged a message pertaining to me, and this knowledge altered my perspective on the outing. I began to feel horror at the thought of meeting the mysterious relatives. An idea seized me with jolting force; the notion that Lisa was ushering me to a slaughter, to my own last rites, a sacrifice that would be performed by this hidden clan. She and I would never get married, and our bruising sex of an hour ago had been a sort of swift finale to the countless nights we had spent together.

We dashed on, the house behind us. The land dipped into the family's apple field. To my sides the trees appeared to be flying backwards and the pendant apples were ball-shaped blurs. Lisa had hunched down in her saddle, jockey fashion, but I was weak and wobbly, a rider hesitant to continue. I no longer had control of my horse. It whisked ahead on the gravel track without any guidance from me, and as if overcome by panic, it ignored my jerks on the reins, my repeated vocal commands. Nothing I did to the colt slowed it, yet it ran with a smoothness and a fluidity that suggested internal calm. Its haste, I realized, emanated not from fear, but from a desire to reach our destination. The horses knew where we were going and I could do nothing but hang onto mine, afraid that a jump to the ground would be fatal.

The woods loomed before us, green, dense, and I smelled the sap on the juniper cones as we sliced through a rift in the wall of pines. Everything darkened. The matted treetops blocked out a view of the sky and the shadows of the wind-blown branches writhed on the soil like phantom snakes. I heard a pheasant gabbling, ducks honking, a rodent squeaking in its den. Our horses managed to negotiate a route through the prickly underbrush and I was amazed they never stumbled, that they maintained their gallop. Thorns seemed not to hurt them, logs they vaulted, and they crossed a marsh without difficulty,

19

as if skimming the water's surface.

"Lisa!" I said her name six times, but she gave me no response. Still in front, still working her bridle, Lisa disregarded my voice or perhaps she could not hear it with the hooves clattering over the twigs and stones.

"Lisa, I'm going to get killed riding like this." We had always gone east or north when we rode from the mansion; those sections of the woods had trails. Like barbed thongs, the limbs with needles lashed my face, and to avoid having my eyes hit, I kept myself down, practically hugging the colt's neck. In its mane, an orange fleece, I could smell its perspiration and this had an acid odor which mingled with the stench of decaying flora, plants that had become casualties of autumn. Lightheaded, I held my breath, then I began to inhale through my mouth. And I had resigned myself to making this trip, to facing Lisa's relatives, people I envisioned as mental defectives or homicidal lepers. Something had to be wrong with them. Why else did the group, the whole tribe, lead such a withdrawn existence?

We came out into the open. From the edge of the woods, the last of the pines, a weedy slope descended towards a lake. Above the water stretched a bridge, rickety planks with spaces between them, and I nodded to myself when I saw that it went to a little island. On that stood a number of decrepit cabins and blackish smoke was rising from their chimneys. Dissipated by the wind, some of the smoke blew over the water and into us, spreading the scent of corn gruel. Apparently it was cooking time for the relatives.

The sky had changed. The silvery brightness in it had dulled, and it seemed to be closer to the earth than before. Steeped in gloom and getting darker, the sky could have been a representation of my mood, and as my horse, trailing Lisa's, trotted down the hill, I glanced up at the columns of fog massing in the west. 'How dreary,' I thought, and lowered my gaze. But the lake disheartened me also. Clotted algae, a pea-green scum, fringed the bank and the floating ring sent up vapors that reminded me of a sewer. In the shallows and on the lily pads frogs were croaking, a sepulchral chorus, and when we moved onto the bridge, we entered a cloud of swirling gnats. Lisa muttered, I swatted the air, and the horses, walking now, stepping from one precarious board to the next, flicked their ears and neighed angrily. "Come on boy," Lisa said, encouraging her stallion. "Careful...easy...we'll give you a drink after this..."

I glimpsed them then, huddled in their doorways, malformed, disfigured. And we proceeded to a clearing among their cabins, a soggy patch where we pulled up. With her usual grace, Lisa dismounted and at her signal, a snap of her fingers, the relatives converged on us, bare feet sloshing through the mire. "Don't just sit there," Lisa said, and I knew that I had to conceal my loathing. Teeth clamped together, I showed them a smile, but behind my grin I suppressed the urge to vomit. My chest swelled and shook, causing an explosion of pain. I fought it, in agony, and everything stayed down. The nausea passed. I kicked up a leg and slipped from the saddle, punched my thighs to combat cramps. Lisa pointed beyond the cabins and leading her horse by the reins, she started to walk towards a trough. The relatives went with us, a mob of gnarled limbs and oblong heads, and I was aware of their scrutiny, their gawking, their dry-voiced whispers. I made it to the trough, stopped beside Lisa, turned my back on every one of them. 'Finish it,' I was thinking. 'Get the sacrifice over with.' And Lisa, showing no signs of tension or expectancy, patted her stallion's nose, inviting it to drink and quench its thirst. The liquid before us was brown and foamy. "Cider," I said, cupping my hands, and I treated myself to a sip. As I swallowed I must have grimaced, for it had a bitter tang that surprised me. Lisa shrugged. "The horses really like it," she said. "Can't get enough when they come here." And I understood why they had been in a hurry to reach the island. When a horse was taken on the arduous ride, its reward for the effort was applejack, and from my taste of what was offered, I gathered that the recluse clan had its own special brew.

Nervous again, I met the stares. The relatives were a slump-shouldered bunch, and I studied their pink and pupilless eyes, the brows without lashes, the bulbous nasal organs through which they wheezed. In their eagerness to observe me, the ones who had been dining had forgotten to wipe their mouths, and yellow corn mush clung to their lips and beards. Though not leprous, as I had suspected, they did have skins marked with all kinds of blemishes: pus, scabs, blisters, lesions and sores. They stank of decomposition and fungal growths. But they meant me no harm, that I could see, and since I had no reason to be afraid, I was able to relax a bit. Only a residual nausea remained, a mucal wedge sitting in my throat like a fishbone.

"Family," said Lisa. "There's nothing like it." She spoke with pride and contentment. Clearly she derived a sense of completeness from being related to so many. The relatives were old, perhaps some were ancient, and Lisa referred to the beauty of knowing that one of these days she, too, would have a cabin on this plot of family land.

"It's wonderful," she said.

"What is?"

"Contact with the family past."

"You mean with them?"

"With them. Having them here, and the intimate contact."

"Wonderful," I echoed.

"And after the wedding you'll truly be part of it."

She gave me a kiss and I did my best not to cringe. I think I was already considering murder. What galled me was Lisa's attitude, her assumption that I would accept these slobbering things as my relations.

"Now for the still," she said. "Follow me."

A buzz went through the assemblage and the slouching figures became our escorts. They shambled beside us like a band of tamed gorillas. Some were talking at normal volume, but I could not begin to comprehend their dialect, a speech so broken and guttural it seemed to be drawn from their intestines. As we marched by the trough, I heard the swishing of a tail and a slurping noise, and between two crookbacked bodies trudging forward, I saw for a second the upraised head of my auburn colt, its ears drooping, its gums exposed, eyes glazed with the mist of intoxication. Then a beetle crashed into my neck, sticking me with its pincers, but before I could grab the bug, it flew off into the air, a black dot against the lowering sky. The fog had thickened, by degrees had crept in from the west, and it was blanketing us with its whiteness. Soon it would enshroud the island, soon it would envelope the woods through which Lisa and I had come, and it might be impossible to get home on the drunken horses. But I was prepared to walk to the house if that would be my sole alternative to spending the night in this abhorrent place.

Lisa brought me past the cabins, and at the crest of a bluff she stepped inside a peak-roofed shanty, the largest building on the island. I ducked through the doorway. The relatives came surging in, collecting against the walls, hunkering down on the hard, dirt floor. Silent except for their respiration, that nasal rasping, they composed an attentive audience, and in the light of the oil-lamp burning on a wooden table they looked even more grotesque than previously; they were lumpish forms, shadows out of a bad dream.

In front of me stood Lisa, declaring that she had a proposal. She prodded my arm and ran her hands along her braid. Intrigued by her forceful tone, I listened to her closely, and at the same time I circled amid the equipment: corked jugs, metal cylinders, gas tanks, a capacious oven-stove. For everything in this room, Lisa said, I would be the one responsible, and when I perceived the nature of her demand, I interrupted her with a statement of compliance. She softened, she beamed at me, and I said several things that confirmed my willingness to do the job. I had helped in the making of regular cider, sold in the region by her parents, so to learn the distillation process would be no major task.

"My father's been doing it for years," she said. "He's getting tired."

"I can't blame him."

"All they need is their liquor, the liquor made here, and they're fine."

"It'll be an honor to make it," I said.

"You can use corn or apples or whatever. Mix it up for them."

"I will," I said.

"You'll really be a good addition to the family," Lisa said. "I can tell already."

"Your blood is my blood. What's a little duty to your own family?"

The monsters banged their fists against the floor, and the squawks and grunts they emitted I took to be their version of cheering. Around the room they straightened up and their blobbish torsos lurched toward me from every side. Their salivating mouths were cavities of joy; in many of the faces the pink eyes glimmered, leaking sentimental tears. Caught in the crush, I froze in my spot and I had to take their pats, their slaps on the back, and a few bear hugs that left me coated with a bloody slime. I shivered all over. I felt my stomach contracting. But I clenched my teeth and battled the wave of nausea, subdued the sick feeling again. "One of us," a voice said, a voice that rose from deep in a throat. "Paul Raven's one of us." And in their midst was Lisa, a grinning Lisa, a Lisa entirely at her ease, put off by neither their odor nor their appearance. She fluttered about, she hopped and pranced in her cowboy boots, she acknowledged the yawps of congratulations regarding the wedding. 'My bride to be,' I thought in disgust, and without any semblance of haste or anger, I wriggled through the press of misshapen bodies and got myself to the door.

In the open air I breathed heavily, relieved to have escaped the putrescent relatives. But now I could smell the lake's fetid vapors, fumes that itched inside my nostrils. I blundered through the murk, the white fog mixed with the chimney smoke, and at the trough with the applejack, the besotted horses nosed up next to me. They nuzzled my chest, playful as ponies, but I used my palms to shove them off. Both the horses drooled and reeled. I kicked my colt's left front leg, infuriated by this drunkenness, and although I did not expect it to budge, I heaved myself onto it and kept on kicking, digging the stirrups into its flanks. I almost hoped that it would collapse, that it would die under my punishment, but instead the animal broke into action. It reared once and started to gallop, and before I could get a grip on the reins, it was off the island and speeding across the dangerous bridge, its hooves somehow finding the planks and missing the spaces between them.

"Paul!"

Somewhere behind me Lisa had yelled. I righted myself in the saddle, found the reins, turned my shoulders and glanced back. All I saw was a female ghost, Lisa's willowy outline in the fog. And from near her came lugubrious groans, an indication that my abrupt departure had offended the relatives. The milky whiteness obscured everything. Yet the colt rumbled on with utter abandon, and the alcohol seemed not to impair its remarkable feel for the woods. Stubborn as before, it ran according to its own will, defying my attempts to restrain it. But as I listened to the rhythm of its thudding feet, to the cracking of twigs and sticks underfoot, I felt an uncanny confidence in the horse and relinquished my desire to wield control. Head low, hands secure on the slack reins, I was swept along as if weightless, and it did not stop running till we reached the stable.

There, in its stall, while it sat panting on a bed of straw, I spoke to the boy who tended the horses. Though simple-minded, the waif had a natural aptitude for what he did. I told him about the apple brandy the colt had consumed. He set to work with his woolen blankets; I scampered across the pebbles and grass heading toward the house. The veil of haze had thickened somewhat and up on the roof, in the spiraling breeze, the rusted cock was gyrating. Wilson, a fanatic for cleanliness, accosted me in the foyer, but I brushed past the servant and ascended the parquet stairs, planting mud with my boots. I went into my bathroom for a shower and underneath the steaming water, I scrubbed and soaped every part of myself, determined to strip off the relatives' slime. Afterwards, I rinsed thoroughly, and I walked over to the medicine cabinet mirror. I put one elbow to the glass, wiped it clear, waited and wiped again. My face, glum as a death mask, came into focus, and I examined the curious conjunction of bones that made it up. Everything in it was out of proportion, the eyes a little too large, the forehead too high, the nose too flat, the mouth too wide for the chin below it. Seen as a whole, the different parts of my face were striking, but in a way that would have pleased a portrait artist more interested in an odd countenance than in a classic type of masculine beauty.

I had inherited this blend of features from my parents, but I could not for the life of me recall what they had looked like. Nor could I remember a single fact about their ancestries, though my tan complexion probably denoted a mixed lineage. From the time I had come to this house, had joined Lisa and her parents, my memories of my mother and father had grown dimmer and dimmer. I could remember virtually nothing of them and this seemed so unnatural that I had to assume that something had been done to me. Drugs? Hypnosis? A doctor paid by the family to meddle with my brain? It did not seem paranoid to think so, and I felt as if I'd been asleep for all the years I'd lived in the house. I had come to love Lisa and her parents, but they had robbed me of my past. I had learned to trust them, but they'd only wanted to empty my mind and fill it with loyalty to them. The years had passed and I had been asleep, but the meeting with the relatives had woken me up. After that visit, I was beginning to understand. I could see what I was to Lisa and her parents, and as I stood before the mirror, I wept for what I had lost.

Knuckles rapped on the bathroom door and I heard the cat meow.

"You alright?" Lisa asked. "Something wrong?"

"Not at all."

"Good. The relatives were glad to meet you. You'll be a success with them."

"We're all family," I said.

But I vowed to myself that I would never make a drop of liquor for the hideous clan.

Chapter Five

It was the eve of the wedding. Lisa and I had decided to sleep in our separate rooms. A night apart would enable us to get a proper rest, and she said that she wanted to look her prettiest for the ceremony. "You can live without me for one night," she said, and at eleven o'clock we touched lips and turned in. For two hours, two interminable hours, I sat in my chair reading, waiting till I was sure that Lisa's parents, and Wilson, had retired. Then I got up and went to my closet, putting on dungarees, my workboots and a black sweatshirt. The door between our rooms was closed but still I moved with the utmost caution lest a noise rouse Lisa, kindle her curiosity. She, if awakened, would call out from the bed; she would ask me what I was doing up. Well, I could say I was going for a walk, and that I preferred to go alone. 'Just can't sleep with all this excitement,' I could say, and I felt certain she would believe me. I had given her no reason to suspect me of anything.

Outside the window a bird came gliding down, an owl with coppery plummage. It landed on the ledge, its talons scraping the wood, and through the gossamer drapes it looked distorted, even spectral. I saw its head spin round on unmoving shoulders, noticed the radiant eyes staring, taking stock of my face. A hostile bird, it seemed to know my present intentions and I rushed toward the windowpane to scare it. The owl hooted, puffing its feathers, and I watched its flapping wings carry it up through the golden moonlight. Behind, on the sill, it had left the torn remains of a mouse.

I switched off the lamp, ready to leave. But against my wiser judgment, possessed by a nostalgic sentiment, I opted for a peek at Lisa. Hand to the knob, I pushed open half the double door, exposing her room to the lunar shafts slanting through mine. She lay face up and in placid repose, her arms outstretched on the majestic four-poster. Was she dreaming, dreaming of a marriage that would last? The eiderdown quilt, the blanket under which we had frolicked so often, covered her legs and slender waist, and where her pajama top had ridden up, I could see her sunken navel. Beneath her head the black mass of hair fanned outwards like a flower arrangement, a floral design on the white sheet, and as I thought of its satiny texture, of the balsam fragrance from her shampoo, I was tempted to kneel by her side, smell her hair, bury my face in that softness. Just imagining the act stimulated me.

Two green eyes emerged from the dark and the Persian cat let out a snarling meow. Legs bent, tail looped, it inched forward on the plush carpet, slid toward me in silence. I would have enjoyed hanging it by its neck, killing it right then for the scratches it had given me, but that would have been too impetuous. 'You'll get yours with the others,' I said, returning its fierce gaze, and I slowly pulled the door shut. There was a thump on the other side. The cat wailed as if in pain and I knew that a second earlier it had leapt at me with claws extended, hitting the door hard.

From my desk I lifted a torch and in the black tunnel of the hall, I kept the beam aimed low. The parquet steps, a turn to the left, another passage, and I had entered the foyer. My rubber-soled boots squeaked on the tiles and at the entrance, the oak portal, the bolt clanked when I tried to ease it loose. 'Son-of-a-bitch,' I muttered. I tightened my fingers, jerked my arm, and got the bolt to give, expecting someone to wake up. But nobody spoke, nobody came to the stairs; in this house they slept like the dead. Wind blew in, wet with drizzle, heavy with the scent of grass and pines, but in my ears I heard something else. I heard a comforting liquid sound like the splashing of waves against a beach. The tropics won't be so bad, I thought. Just have to improve my French. I should've been more serious about it when I had it in school.

I left the door open a crack and ran past the front of the stable. Two or three horses reacted, bucking in their stalls, lashing at the hay, and the boy who fed and trained them, lying on his pallet in the loft, moaned. I stopped at once, but nothing resulted from this commotion and the horses calmed down. Legs churning, I hurried on, and over at the tool shed I reached into my pocket for my keys. Everything smelled of oil and moss inside, and using the torch I edged through shovels and hoes, clippers and spades, the fertilizer bags and the vats of insect poison. I had to pick apart a spider's web, white glutinous filaments, to get my bicycle from the corner, and after I had wrung my hands clean of the fibers, I rolled the ten-speed out to the yard. Climbing on, I felt resistance in the peddles and gears.

But I had enough air in the tires, the brakes worked and the bike's headlight still functioned, old as it was. 'It'll do,' I said, squeezing the corroded handlebars. 'It's not fancy, but it'll do.'

I bumped over the gravel embankment; I pedalled onto the rough road linking the estate to the nearest town. I had the force of the wind against me, the wind and the blistering rain. I had the holes and the puddles to contend with and the clouds hid all but a piece of the circular moon, leaving me just the one thin beam of the bicycle lamp shining down on the asphalt. Already my thighs throbbed from this exertion, and though the air was cool, I felt hot. My every breath a burning rip in my lungs, I wanted to rest, to pull off the pavement and shelter myself under a tree in the woods, but Larry would be angered if I arrived late. For his help in this matter, I could only be grateful and I owed him the courtesy of being on time. So I marshalled my strength and kept myself going, pushed myself in spite of dizziness. There was the insistent cricket chirping, the hammering of the rain, the wind in my face. But at least the storm, which had not been predicted, served as an effective cover; in weather this harsh the chances of my meeting someone were slim - and that was good. People in the area knew about the imminent marriage and anyone who saw me cycling tonight would have to think it peculiar.

Where the road curved left, I went straight, absorbing shocks from several ruts. I passed the big chalky boulder and hit the cement track into Graveyard Ravine. Branches closed over me, an arc of wilting foliage, and I took the descent coasting, bending into the upswirls of air. At the bottom was the cemetery, a burial ground for the whole district, and beyond that the turbid waters of Graveyard Creek. I applied pressure to the brakes, hearing the skid of the tires, and on the grass beside the pond I came to a gradual stop, happy to see the tan coupe. The motor was off, the inside light turned on; through the water streaming down the passenger window I saw an arm in a baggy sleeve extending toward the door. When the lever clicked, the door swung open and a skeletal hand beckoned me in. "Come on," Larry said. "The car's getting soaked." And I let the bike fall and got in fast, slamming the door, shaking myself.

"You could put on the heat," I said.

Larry started the ignition and then the blower. I listened to the rain and felt the warmth gushing in through the vents. Submitting to my fatigue, I sat limp on the ragged vinyl and I wished I could dry my sodden clothes, change my socks and boots. The droplets were smacking against the windshield like silver pellets.

"You didn't have trouble finding the place?"

"None," said Larry. "The little fork at the white boulder. Your directions were perfect."

He had ketchup on his chin and the smell of the burger he had just finished eating remained in the car. Soda cans strewn on the floor, candy wrappers stuffed in the cigarette dish, paperbags from junk food restaurants scattered in the back. This was the same Larry I had always known, the Larry who had visited me five times at the estate and who, on each occasion, had exasperated Lisa's parents with his sloppiness. But he was an old friend, a buddy since childhood, since the years I had lived in Manhattan, and I would have trusted nobody else as my confederate.

"What?" I said, for he was talking and he had a somber edge in his voice.

"I really don't like the rain," he said. "It gives me the aches."

He meant in his jaw, in the damaged nerves of his face. Doctors had performed three operations since the accident he had gone through, and though their work had removed the scars, he would forever have a crooked, sneering mouth and a scarcely perceptible twitch in his left cheek. Dank weather, so he said, infused the area with a painful stiffness, a soreness assuaged only by his prescribed tablets. And he said he needed two of the tablets now but would have to wait till he reached the hotel because the codeine in them made him too drowsy to drive.

"This damn rain. You don't think it will screw things up tomorrow?'

"The wedding won't be cancelled," I said.

"That's not what I mean."

"Well..." I paused, considering what I would do if the rain continued for another day. "No," I said. "The marriage is set and if what you brought me is good, it won't make a difference rain or shine."

He whirled in his seat, fuzzy red hair close to my face, gaunt arms stretching toward the rear, and when he turned to the front again, he laid a blue rucksack on my lap. With his surly lips and the fiery squint in his steel-grey eyes, he somehow conformed in my mind to the image of a terrorist.

I unzipped the sack and inspected the bombs and Larry explained how I was to rig up the timers.

"I wrote it all down for you just in case."

"And the guy who put all this together?"

"Don't worry about him," Larry said.

"He didn't ask questions?"

"He delivered what I asked and that's it."

"And the money? No problem with that?"

"None. The amount you wired covered everything."

The wind had slackened but the rain kept coming. That hamburger smell mingled with the car's mustiness began to irritate me, and in the hope of breathing fresher air, I cranked my window down a bit. "Nuts!" I said, for I had forgotten the creek was a pool where local authorities dumped the people too poor to afford a graveyard burial. The bodies spawned a sickening odor and from the woods came the smell of fallen leaves and rotting ferns, autumnal death. Yet, once the nature in the Hudson basin had seemed so alive and magical; once I had romped through the groves like a merry faun. A single day, the day at the lake, at the island with Lisa's relatives, had tainted the region for me, had made me overly aware of the physical corruption going on every place. Would a new domicile in the tropics, in an unfamiliar world, rid me of this morbid perception? Without comment, I rolled up the window.

"You got my ticket for Martinique?"

"At home," said Larry. "I got it. You'll fly to Antigua and switch there."

So the preparations were complete. Now I could return to the house and set the explosives and by tomorrow night I would be on the move.

"It's funny in a way," I said. "Her parents just added a wing to the mansion."

"Really? What for?"

"Our wedding present. We're to see the inside tomorrow and then we're supposed to have it all to ourselves."

"Nothing's done yet," said Larry. "You don't have to go through with this."

"I know. But I'm not going to be a slave making that special liquor for the relatives. Shit. If I married her that's what I'd be, even with all the comforts. I'd be a goddamned servant for those monsters."

Larry responded with a laugh, a misanthrope's chuckle.

31

"You really think they adopted you just for that?"

"I do."

"They wanted you to work for them?"

"That's what I'm saying."

"Bastards," he said.

I had to admit that Lisa's endearments toward me seemed genuine. But when I had hinted after my initial agreement that I might be less than enthusiastic minding the relatives' still, producing their supply of life-supporting liquor, when I had said that I intended to marry her and not some tedious job, she had leveled an ominous glare at me, an expression that brooked no compromise. That evening, at dinner, she reported my complaints to her parents and the couple I had known as generous wards also became implacable. Who had kept me out of the orphanage? they said. Who had raised me as their own child and sent me to college? With this marriage I was to become a full-fledged member of their family, and as part of my responsibility to the family, I would have to do work for the respected relatives. "You'll be in their position one day," Lisa's father said. "You and all the rest of us here. We'll be drinking the special booze a descendant's making for us. Maybe your son will have the honor."

From the yard rose a racket of gurgling voices and I walked to the dining room window. In the pallid moonlight I saw the monsters for the second time, saw them lugging their wasted carcasses over the grass, saw them sliding and lurching and shifting on the grass, saw them craning their necks to get a look at me, their pupilless eyes become red disks. "I've done it for years," Lisa's father was saying. "And I've been proud to serve this family. All we want is for you to replace me. You're much younger, much fitter, and it has to be a man tied to the family by marriage or blood. That's the tradition."

"They can't make the liquor themselves?"

"The very thought!" he said, almost gagging on his words. "The very idea of putting our ancestors to work."

And so they had ensnared me. They'd taken me in when I lost my parents and let the bond between Lisa and me grow stronger. I knew why now, and for all the luxuries they had provided, I felt used and deceived.

"Okay," I said, and turned from the window, revolted by the sight of the relatives. "I understand. Of course I do. I just had a moment of doubt. Nerves."

"Forget it," Lisa's father said. "You're still my son."

"And you, all of you, my family."

"Then on with the wedding!" Lisa said.

I puckered my lips and blew her a kiss. But I was thinking of escape, or some form of revenge, or I could escape after I had revenge and for any help I might need I could probably get Larry...I could telephone Larry...

"Lar'," I said, watching the rain as it splashed down into the creek of corpses. "I have a question for you."

"What?"

"Do you remember what my parents looked like?"

"Your parents?"

"Their faces..anything. Because I can't seem to remember them."

"You weren't that young when they got killed."

"I know that, but..."

"Don't you have pictures?"

"No." I said.

"They were *your* parents," he said. "Not mine."

With a jab at the dashboard, a touch of a button, he set the windshield wipers in motion, and as I listened to them go, the monotony of their sound became soothing.

"Right," I said. "I better shove off. Lots to do while it's still dark."

"Good luck."

"Good luck yourself. Just get to your hotel and be at the estate tomorrow."

Outside the coupe I strapped on the rucksack. The little bulb in the car went out, the tires dug into the dirt and grass, and I heard the sputtering of the engine as Larry drove up the hill. Seated on the bike, I began my laborious ascent from the ravine, but during this trip I felt no fatigue. I ignored the rain and the chafing wetness of my clothes, and the explosives, secure in the sack, were no burden at all.

'Bombs away,' I said to myself. 'I'm blowing your fucking family sky high.'

Chapter Six

Here in Martinique it can get claustrophobic living in this dingy room. During those times I see the walls bulging, closing in on me, and faced with the conviction that I will suffocate, I have to go out. I go to the beach and lie in the sun, or I begin one of my random jaunts around Fort de France. Often I find myself in a bar and I drink until I regain my composure. But even then, when I have vanquished the shameful panic and can accept a return to the confinement of my room, I cannot prevent myself from remembering the new wing of the mansion that Lisa's parents showed us on our wedding day. With what pride, what delirious pride, did they usher us through that spacious addition to the house. With what effusive gestures did they point at the rich velvety curtains, the brilliant chandeliers, the impeccable English china, the wine glasses from Venice, the black and white marble floors. We had a kitchen the size of a restaurant's and upstairs ('Oh, my!' said Lisa) a collection of rooms crammed with lavish furnishings. "Will it do?" said Lisa's mother. "Do you like it?" And Lisa, crying with gratitude, hugged each of her parents while I told them I could never dream of having a better home than this one.

We had been married that afternoon. The ceremony was done by a judge in town. Then we had driven back to the estate and after our tour of the new wing, the relatives had met us in the parlor. I survived the carousing, the family celebration, and by evening, when Lisa and I made our exit, the monsters lay on the couches and floor, their stomachs bloated, chins and beards streaked with saliva. They had drunk themselves silly, just as I had thought they would, and none would be going to their island tonight. All was well; everything on schedule.

Candles were burning in our room and on the table beside the bed stood a bottle of iced champagne. I twisted the wire and popped the cork and when the fizz came spurting out, I asked Lisa to make the toast. She suggested we drink to a lifelong union, to health, prosperity and our future children, and slow as I could, I poured the champagne into our glasses. Lisa flushed, a girl high on her own joy, and after we had gone bottoms up, she said she wanted a kiss. I gave her one. A long tongue-to-tongue kiss and Lisa toed off her silver heels. At her throat she had a diamond brooch, on her wrists she wore sapphire bands, and the tortoise shell clasp in her braided hair reflected the orange of the candles.

"Lisa," I said, "My sister and wife. My lover, Lisa." For I was feeling an unrepressable sadness and she did look magnificent in her bridal gown. Beginning to stoop, I grabbed her hips and I rubbed my face through the frills and sequins, the exquisite taffeta.

"Tear it," she said. "Tear it off. I won't be needing it again." And while her hands clawed at my scalp, ruffled the woolly thickness there, I seized the gown above her breast and did as she had asked. I pulled the fabric off her shoulders and down her waist, down to her feet and the black carpet. We sank to the rug, I on top, and for a split second I glanced up at the luminescent dial on the bedside clock. It was eight p.m., so I'd have three hours to spend with her. Rarely had I been as charged or urgent. I wanted to use every minute we had to relish her body for the last time. Lisa was lithe, she was by turns submissive and aggressive, and with my hands and mouth, I re-explored her curves and hollows, telling myself, 'Remember her neck, remember the cords of muscle in it. Remember her firm, rounded shoulders. Remember her breasts and the way they taste, her buttocks and how it felt to squeeze. Remember the black curls over her sex, and do remember their oozing moistness, the musky smell.' Because on this night, this one night, Lisa was less a person to me than a combination of alluring parts, and I was determined never to forget those parts. We reached a climatic point, we rested, we began again. We thrust to another culmination and polished off the champagne, and yet again we recommenced, unable to tire ourselves out.

"You're a whirlwind tonight," said Lisa, purring, and I told her that my ardor was due to the occasion, the wedding.

She dozed on the rug while I reminisced. I recalled our horseback journeys through the woods, our nude baths in rushing streams, the times we had ventured into scary caves pretending we would dig up treasure, and I marveled at my own steadfastness as the moment of destruction approached. With nothing to do but wait, I looked across the room at the pleated curtains, stared for a while at the bluish moon. Lisa had flipped onto her side and one of her arms, baby-pink, lay across my chest.

"Lisa," I said, pinching her wrist. "You have to answer me something."

She yawned once and came up into a semi-lotus position. The front of her hair, the unbraided portion, had become dissheveled, and her smile was sheer tenderness. When I noticed that, the love in her face, I bit my tongue to keep from speaking, but the pressure of the passing seconds goaded me on. I could not dawdle knowing that the bombs were soon to explode.

"You have to explain why I can't remember my parents," I said. "Practically nothing about them."

The bleariness lifted from her eyes and I felt Lisa going tense.

"Your parents." I said. "They were the ones. Or they brought in a doctor to help them do it."

And Lisa said nothing; she uttered neither a denial of my statements nor a conflicting explanation. My brusque tone had caught her by surprise and she knew that her parents, or a specialist they had engaged, had brainwashed me sometime after my adoption. Someone had tampered with my mind so that I would have no recollections of my parents, no images of them in my memory. "I can see why," I said. "Easier to make me accept your family as my own. To get me to accept your relatives and the work you want me to do for them. Well, it didn't succeed. Not quite. It's true I can't picture my parents, and yours must've destroyed the photos I had of them, but you haven't won me over. You almost did, but when we went to see those relatives I woke up. Seeing them, seeing that you want me to be their slave - that brought me out of it. I'm not your slave. I'm not going to be at the beck and call of monsters. Sorry, Lisa. I love you, but sorry."

I reached to the left and groped through my clothes. From the pouch inside my tuxedo jacket I drew the knife with the retractable blade. Lisa started to rise, gasping in bewilderment, but I jumped to my feet before she could escape. The pull of the weapon across her throat muffled her attempted scream and I held her down while the blood flowed out, held her until the convulsions ceased. Then a set of claws hooked onto my back and I heard twangy mewling, feline sobs. The Persian, ever-watchful, had sprung from somewhere in the room, and I had to send my hand up and over my shoulder, poking at the distraught beast. It plopped to the rug and I spun and kicked, knocked it flying into the wall. In moments, I was dressed, clad in my wedding apparel sans the tie and jacket, and on my way toward the door I paused next to Lisa, struck by a craving for a souvenir, a momento of what she had once meant to me. Kneeling, I retrieved the knife from where I had left it on the carpet, and with the bloodstained edge, I cut off her Indian braid. I put the silken strand to my nose, smelled the balsam in it, shoved it into my pants pocket. And I also took her diamond brooch and sapphire bracelets, since they could be converted into currency.

Down the hall and steps I went, and I passed the snoring heaps in the parlor. The night was warm and luminous, the horses and the stable boy made no sounds as I jogged across the lawn, and at the rim of the property, the beginning of the public road, Larry was sitting in his tan coupe, one arm jutting out the driver's window.

"Is it done?"

"She's dead. That's for sure."

Ten minutes later the air flashed white, the three explosions simultaneous. Blinded for an instant, I shied in the seat and the roaring crackle of the blaze filled my ears. The original mansion had collapsed. The roof of the new wing caved in, and as flames engulfed the structure, relatives staggered across the yard trailing fire from their rags. Like humans they shrieked, like humans they fell, and their flesh burnt off in sizable chunks, smoking afterwards in the grass. Some of the monsters would live, yes; but who would be around to make their liquor? Not Lisa, that I knew, and her parents had been sleeping very close to one of the bombs.

We drove away.

*****

In his apartment in the Bronx, Larry put a sheet and a blanket on his couch and there for two straight nights I slept. I was busy otherwise, buying in Manhattan a suitcase worth of clothes and a trunkload of books. The payments to the man who had constructed the bombs had badly depleted my inheritance money (the one thing of mine Lisa and her parents had never been able to touch), but at a shop in the jewelry district, I managed to get a substantial price for the diamond brooch and the sapphire bracelets. On the morning of my flight, Larry took me to the airline terminal and there were no complications when

I presented my passport and my ticket. As the plane rose into the gunmetal sky, heading south and over the ocean, I bid farewell to New York City, just as I had years earlier, and once again I readied myself for a new abode, a new environment.

'Sun and sea, here I come.'

*****

So I'm in Martinique, in this dilapidated residence, and I have to admit that I do have an ordered life. Bar men know me; I buy the *International Herald Tribune* from the same vendor several times a week; I frequent the outdoor markets for my fruits and vegetables, and five minutes away from here is a large store where I can purchase whatever else I need. Two of my pupils drive to the residence for their English lessons; the others I see in their homes, getting to them on foot or by *taxi collectif*.

Though I can save nothing from what I earn, the teaching provides a dependable income and I have pocket change for movies and for the occasional splurge at a good restaurant. How do I pass the rest of the time? Often I wonder about that myself. One of the numerous idlers in this place, I sit in my shorts and participate in the domino games, or I laze around on the long, shaded balcony that overlooks the public park. The flora below is green and purple, the mango trees have grown tall, and a limpid pond lies adjacent to an open-air rotunda. On the paved footpaths the marijuana sellers gather, rasta guys, and as I relax in my hammock, slung from the roof overhanging the balcony, as I loll there reading, snoozing, sipping wine, I can smell the smoke from their joints and hear them conversing in Creole.

The heat is constant, the sky pastel blue. On my skin the sweat builds up, clinging, grimy. The church clock in the center of town strikes every hour, car horns honk in the streets, and on one of the park benches is the saxophone man, practicing his scales and running through his one song, a jazzy tune. In the mornings I awaken to his halting strains and when the sun begins to set, he slinks off without a word. Never mind that this has been going on since I moved into the residence; never mind that the man's playing has yet to improve. I'm sure he enjoys himself and I hardly even hear his sax anymore, so accustomed to it have I become. And thus the days pass, one exactly like the next, until the fat woman from the management slips the request for the rent underneath my door and I realize that another month has gone by.

It could be the heat, or this lack of anything much to do, but I am frequently stricken with fatigue. At its worst, the fatigue paralyzes me and I spend hours lying in my room with the air conditioner on. I tell myself to get up, get dressed, do something. But I fail to act on my own admonitions. During the day Fort de France is mobbed with people shopping, islanders in from their villages and tourists fresh off the cruise ships, and the old narrow streets become choked with traffic, lines of little French cars. As I think of the sweltering air filled with soot, of the slow moving pedestrians who block your path on the sidewalks, I lose all desire to tread across town and catch the ferry that would take me to the nearest decent beach.

Recumbent on my mattress, I read a detective novel or a book of travel accounts, and when my eyes start to ache, I close the volume and daydream, speculating on how my situation would be different had my parents never been killed. Should I return to New York City? Would I resolve anything by visiting their graves? A pilgrimage to their tomb and inquiries made among their former friends might help set my mind on the course to remembering them. But even if I did undo the effects of Lisa's parents' brainwashing, I would be quite the same as I am now - that is, alone and adrift, *un homme solitaire*. And by this time, as Larry has informed me, the police in New York State know that I am missing. The story of the bombing in the Hudson basin appeared in the newspapers, and according to what he wrote in his letters, the medical specialists identified the bodies found in the debris. Larry is safe, unsuspected, but for me an arrest warrant exists. I am one of the hunted, the notorious. My sensational deed, I would bet, has been the subject of discussion up and down the Hudson Valley. To re-enter the country on a false passport might be possible, but is the risk worth it? I would rather be here than in prison.

Yes, Martinique beats jail. Until I have the money to depart (and go where? Some place not an island, some place less confining), I must try to be moderately content. I must take my pleasures where I find them; in a morning cup of *cafe au lait*, in a warm loaf of French bread, in the smell of the sea and the extraordinary color of the flowers. Yes, for the languishing exile, Martinique offers consolations. I just wish I could connect with its strutting beauties, the models of chic fashion and patrician *hauteur,* because a monk's rigor, celibacy, is hard to tolerate after the years of sexual exercise with Lisa. I still have the braid I took that night and caressing it, fondling it, putting it under my nose, does spur me towards a physical release. The herbaceous odor contained in the black threads reminds me of Lisa in all her sensuality, her carnal profusion; but it also brings me back to those difficult seconds when I slit her jugulars. At times I simply cannot touch the woven string of hair and I have to seek out Charles, my bilingual friend. On his boat anchored by the waterfront bar, I sit in the cabin and watch his pornographic videos, loathing them even as I reach for the box of tissues. "See you soon" I say when finished, and I step onto the dock. From the shadows at the bow, Charles mutters *au revoir* and he continues to gaze up at the stars, another person who dreams of escaping the island. Obviously he could sail off in his boat, we could embark together, but he has an obsessive concern for his sister and her afflictions. He refuses to leave her behind and knows that taking her along would be infeasible. Unlike me, Charles has let his familial ties become shackles, and for this I pity him.

It is after midnight when I quit the harbor area. Fort de France is a ghost town. The people in the residence have retired to their rooms. I plod down the ill-lit hall toward mine, and through one of the doors I hear kissing and a girl's mischievious laughter. The Guadeloupian in Number Ten is burning his incense, the fragrance a sweet narcotic. Around a corner and at the end of the passage, I come to my own door and I see that the paper with my name written on it has fallen to the carpet. I go inside and grab my roll of transparent tape; I re-attach the white card. It says that I, Paul Raven, live in this room and thus it has importance for me. It signifies my possession of this deteriorated cell and helps me think of the space as home, albeit a temporary one. The chipped wooden table, the ugly metal wardrobe frame, the armless chair and the bed with rattling springs - yes, I have shoddy furniture and, yes, I have no adornments, no decorations, just the blank yellow walls and curtains with faded designs, but undoubtedly I feel pride for having adapted to these Spartan conditions, I who have always known nothing but the womb of luxury. Still, enough is enough. I have to get my hands on some money. Lethargic though I am, I am not unobservant and I keep watching and waiting, sniffing the winds, looking for an opportunity by which I can benefit. There will be one eventually and when I spot it, I will pounce.

Like a spider in its web, I lie dormant yet alert, anticipating the arrival of prey. And when that prey bumbles into my range, I will do whatever I must to overwhelm it. I may have to be brutal in the process, but after the murder and the bombing, I know that I am capable of anything. Nothing, no type of crime, is beyond me now.

The spider waits.

PART TWO

Chapter Seven

Raven heard the voices before he saw the pair. Out in the hall beyond his door a man and a woman with American accents kept repeating the words, 'Bus. Where catch bus for the north? Bus,' as if they were teaching English to an imbecile. Their labored diction carried a note of false deference and they seemed to believe that the louder they asked their question, the more they would improve their chances of extracting an intelligible answer. But the male voice responding to them remained unhelpful, insisting in French that its owner did not comprehend their language.

"He knows what the word 'bus' means."

"He doesn't, Eric."

"We should have kept the car another day."

"And return it how before the plane takes off?"

Raven went into the corridor, his chest and feet uncovered, a wet towel around his waist. The Martinican guy, a student at the island's university, glanced toward him like a person rescued from a police interrogation, and with a soft but decisive chop he cleaved an opening between the couple and sought the sanctuary of his room. The two heads turned, the eyes blinked in vague confusion, the man tried his luck with Raven, using his hands as suggestive aids.

Raven said, "The buses going north leave from the waterfront. You know the big street that passes the harbor?"

Wariness became grinning relief and the Americans walked up the hall to Raven, their sandals flapping against the carpet. The woman was large but solid, the man a gray-topped spindle, and each of the middle-aged faces had been reddened by the sun.

"You speak good English," said the man, surprised. Raven told them he was from the United States. The smiles widened; now the eyes trained on him shone with friendliness. "I'm Eric and this is my wife, Caroline." Raven shook the mottled hand put forth by Eric, and feeling that he had committed himself to helping them, he offered to escort them to the bus they wanted.

"Thanks," said Caroline. "That would be nice of you."

"He doesn't have to get all dressed for us," said Eric.

"No big deal," said Raven. "Glad to help."

"You've helped already. I know where you mean. Just tell us how to go from this part of town."

Caroline bent over scratching her thigh. Raven looked at the swirly mass of blonde hair, the freckled arm working like a piston, the purplish blot of an insect bite just beneath the hem of her beige shorts. A radio was on inside the residence, the station playing a zouk song with a blood-quickening tempo, and when Caroline had finished scratching her leg, she moved about in time to the music.

"We haven't even gone dancing here," she said to Eric.

"That's one thing avoided."

"How could we come to the Caribbean and not go dancing?"

"Very easily," he said and turned back to Raven. "I hate dancing. I'm as hip as anyone my age, but I just don't like dancing. You have those directions?"

Raven went with them to the balcony gate, talking the whole while. Eric let himself and Caroline through and after he had locked the gate with his key, he thanked Raven for the information and invited him out for evening drinks. "We're in Number Six," he said. "Stop by." Raven promised he would. Eric said, "I hope so," as if he suspected that Raven would snub them, and he declared that he and his wife would enjoy it if Raven accompanied them to dinner. The both of them were hip, he said; the both of them were adventurous, and he ridiculed the typical older types who came to the tropics simply to wallow in the plushness, the baroque decor, of the hotels.

"We have a daughter about your age and she loves to do things with us."

"See you later then," said Raven, a little defensive, and with the ends of her index fingers, Caroline lowered the huge sunglasses that had been nestled in her hair. She set the shades on the bridge of her nose and thus hid what he thought he had seen - a glacial fury in her eyes. A stolid presence in the dark lenses, Caroline began to walk away, forcing her husband to catch up, and whatever Raven had glimpsed in her, if in fact it had been there at all, was gone.

"Till tonight," said Raven. "I'm looking forward to it."

*****

The waiter brought over his round, black tray and put it

down upon their table. As the lanky man spread their things before them - a bottle of beer and a glass for Eric; a Scotch and soda for Caroline; dark rum, sugar cane syrup, and a triangle of lime for Raven - another waiter inside the bar yelled something angrily, a Creole phrase that Raven knew as a vulgar insult. Out through the doorless entrance shot a man in rumpled clothes, and at the curb he pitched headlong into the street. The customers sitting at the sidewalk tables watched him fall, but few if any evinced concern. Locals recognized the bulky drinker; he was a Fort de France vagrant who got himself ejected from bars quite often. Unhurt, his bearded face a goofy smile, the lush picked himself up and with neither shame nor refinement in his bearing, he stepped across the curb to Raven's table. He extended his hand. On rising he had spotted the tourists, Eric and Caroline, had singled them out as sources of money. "L'argent," he said, staring at Caroline, and in this succinct demand he managed to convey swagger. He seemed to expect these visitors to placate him with coins, and his oil-black fingers wiggled with impatience. "Vouz avez l'argent pour moi?"

He slouched above them with his odor of garbage cans and public benches and the waiter who had served them tried to shoo him down the block. Unruffled, the tramp refused to budge and as if giving a clue to what he wanted to buy, what he wanted to do tonight, he playfully flaunted his rotund belly, the tumid flesh, showing where the buttons of his shirt had popped. "Pretty fat for a panhandler," said Eric. "He ain't starving." The man's effrontery was making him laugh, but Caroline, her face ashen, hugged her pocketbook to her breast. And when the man coughed, spitting phlegm, Raven rose in a burst of temper and shouted his own expletives - a few choice words in French. Unaccustomed to such ferocity, to antagonism this threatening, the vagrant withdrew his arm and retreated, backpedaled, vanished around the nearby corner. Raven sat, mumbling curses, and poured himself his ti-punch. There was silence at the other tables, flabbergasted looks, and then the spirited talk resumed, the joking and arguing, the revelry of Friday night drinking. The waiter had gone inside with his empty tray.

"Sorry," said Raven. "But that guy...he reminded me of some people I knew. Creatures really. They were disgusting parasites."

He drank his ti-punch while Caroline dug through her bag.

45

Eric licked the bubbles off his beer. A layer of the foam spilled, leaving a pool on the black ceramic tabletop, and Raven saw Caroline lifting a cigarette, putting it to her mouth with a trembling hand. As it dangled there, stuck to the rim of her lower lip, Caroline dug through her purse again, and up from the black leather depths came her lighter, the fluid visible in the pink tube. A pencil of flame appeared, the fag end sizzled, and she took three or four puffs in rapid succession.

"I'm too high strung," she explained. "It's my temperament."

"Yoga," said Eric. "That's the key. You do that for awhile and..."

A young man burnt fig brown detached himself from cronies on the sidewalk and waving a cigarette in front of Caroline, he pointed at her lighter. His Gaelic face descended on Caroline; her thumbnail spun the combustible rollers; his nostrils flared and his cheeks hollowed as he drew in the smoke.

"It's guaranteed to reduce your tension. I was a bundle of nerves myself until I discovered yoga."

The French youth cocked his head listening to Eric, but it was apparent that he had never learned English. Eric went on describing the advantages of yoga, his fingers a steeple beneath his chin, his gaze fixed on his golden beer as if it were a fount of spiritual secrets, and Caroline, looking at Raven, made a face of utter vacuity, cerebral emptiness. Raven laughed with restraint, with as much civility as he could muster, and the youth discharged a stream of smoke, blowing it into Caroline's eyes. "Did you see that?" she said. "The goddamned creep." She recoiled, dragged her chair back from the table, and even though Raven saw what was happening, the young man lunging, Caroline ducking, flesh slapping against flesh, he continued to laugh for one incongruous moment. The humorous mood of a second before was still with him. That mirth soured and he stood up, striking out in Caroline's defense, but now the youth had hopped beyond his reach, the pink lighter protruding from his hand. He and his circle of skinny friends ran into the street and across the path of an oncoming car, and from the opposite sidewalk, ignoring the blast of the horn behind them, they scooted over a stone rise and entered the public park called the Savane.

"What are we tonight?" said Caroline. "A charity service?"

Strolling people and the bushes at the edge of the park cut

Raven's view of the thief and his companions, but he could visualize them running across the wide field within, running and hollering under the palm trees. Would it pay for him to pursue them? His legs felt leaden and his stomach was chock-full of food; the dinner that Eric and Caroline had treated him to during the evening had been a five-course meal: onion soup, tossed salad, mushrooms sauteed in wine, a lamb couscous plate and for dessert, coconut ice cream. A feast like this he could not have afforded on his own, but in return for their generosity was he supposed to become Caroline's knight? She had only lost a lighter, and a cheap disposable one at that, and if he somehow caught the group, he would be facing terrible odds in a prospective scrap.

"Forget it, Paul," Caroline said, as if she knew what he was considering. "Pour yourself another rum."

She smiled at him while turning her eyes toward her husband, and Raven felt the table buck. Eric winced, clutching for his knee or his shinbone, and it must have been this, the pain from her kick, that brought him out of his meditative trance.

"What's with you?" he asked his wife. "What's gotten you so pissed?" And Raven could see the contempt in her face, the dissatisfaction, the familiarity she had with her husband's obtuseness. Saying nothing, she raised her half-full glass, and at one gulp she finished the Scotch and soda.

"I can't know what it is unless you tell me," Eric said.

But Caroline gave her attention to her cigarette. She smoked and smoked, and she arched one leg over the thigh of the other, fidgeting in her jeans. Some of the color had drained from her skin, some of the shininess from her tan, and Raven saw the years suddenly, the minute wrinkles stretching down from beneath the corners of her nose. Had Eric been, or was he now, a jealous husband? For even these telltale marks of age had not rendered his wife unattractive; she had symmetrical cheekbones, greenish eyes, a curl of insouciance in her lip. There must have been times when Eric had seen men make advances at her, but someone as self-absorbed as him could not possibly be that possessive.

"You're sulking again," said Eric, leaning back in his chair, and with a conspiratorial nod he winked at Raven, reducing the situation to a joke.

"She can get real sulky at home," he said. "Especially with Bianca gone."

"She likes it in Martinique, your daughter?"

"Loves it. Absolutely loves it."

"I'll have to visit her sometime."

"You should. She's in Fort de France. I'll give you the address to her apartment."

In the lane straight down from the bar the Savane food concessions were busy. People were milling around the trucks and reading the chalk-written boards tacked up high. From van to van the menus did not vary: hamburgers, french fries, conch on a skewer, a piece of chicken or fish served with rice. As usual, the one stand selling paella had lured the biggest crowd, and at the crepe truck a man took the orders while a woman with muscular arms ladled out the eggy batter, always spreading it thin and smooth on the two ringed stoves, always folding the crepes easily with her stainless steel spatula.

Perched on the low stone wall bordering the park, seated at the plastic tables under the tents and canopies, the customers ate with paper forks, drank their sodas and beers from the bottle or the can. Napkins fluttered to the pavement; the whirring generators spewed white smoke that smelled of iron and sulphur; around the Savane the moving cars emitted the pulsations of zouk, such festive music, party music. It was a typical scene of Friday night conviviality, but for Raven it could have been happening behind a curtain, an invisible scrim, that barrier which kept him in his isolation. Even tonight, when he had company, he felt locked inside himself and the carping between Eric and Caroline depressed him. Their marriage, an excuse for daily contention, made solitary life seem irresistable.

"Either of you like reggae?" he asked. "I know a good place we can listen to some."

"With dancing? Do they have dancing?" Caroline had perked up, begun to smile, and one of her hands was fiddling with the shiny wooden beads strung from her neck.

"Sure they do," said Raven. "There's dancing."

"Then let's go. We're flying home tomorrow and I wanted to get in a night of dancing."

She mashed the stub of her cigarette out in a red saucer filled with butts. From her purse she took some change, and jangling the coins in her fist she went into the bar to pay the check at the counter. Eric guzzled the rest of his beer, the glass tipped upside down to his mouth, and when Caroline returned to the table, he rose, stretching his arms in an acquiescent shrug.

"Don't complain," she said. "You can sit in a corner and have another beer."

"Or a joint." Raven said.

"I can get pot there?"

"It's a reggae place. What do you think?"

Eric hesitated, stroking his chin. "There was a time when I loved pot," he said. "I never was without it in the house and I would be high almost every day. What a time that was.."

"Before he became crazy for yoga," said Caroline. "Before he became a pseudo-ascetic."

"Pseudo? Because I drank a little the last week? You gotta do that. This is the Caribbean."

"And what will your guru think?"

"Nothing. He won't know."

"You see. A real mystic."

She ran a black comb through her hair, picking at a tuft above her ear, rearranging the patch in front, and with the help of her free hand, which she used like a roller, she sculpted the blonde swirl until she had it seductively unbalanced.

"In case I find me a boyfriend," she said, her lips crinkled demurely. "I might stay behind tomorrow."

With Raven leading, they set off, and Caroline began to chatter about a reggae club she had once gone to in Los Angeles.

They walked across Fort de France and then over one of the bridges on the canal. Orange skins, milk cartons and crumpled yogurt containers floated in the ribbon of smelly water drifting out to sea, and the short-throated lamps lining the sluice illuminated the fish darting around beneath the surface, snapping and tussling for edible garbage. From an intersection at the bottom of a hill, Raven led Eric and Caroline right, and as they started the steep climb, a motorcycle came racing down with two rasta guys on the seat. Though they all scattered, Eric was nearly hit and the passenger rider waved at them, his long dreadlocks streaming. Undisturbed, Raven walked on, but neither Eric nor Caroline during their week on the island had accustomed themselves to avoiding the madcap drivers. They stopped in the road as if another step forward would mean their deaths and Raven saw they were both staring up, surveying the hill and its shadows.

Far behind lay the center of Fort de France, the boulevards that they knew, and everything in this terraced section of twisting alleys and cut-off streets had the ramshackle look of a slum. The dark houses to their sides were thrown together from a hodgepodge of materials - wood, cement, brick, tin - and in the cramped yards, under the hanging clothes and linen, were jagged heaps of junk. Raven realized that he had established no basis of trust with Eric and Caroline. They did not know him well. He had told them he was a master's student at the university, but in their eyes he might be a hustler or a drug addict, a dangerous tropical straggler. In their imaginations he might have shady connections here, friends just waiting to fleece a couple of American tourists. But they had not seemed suspicious of him until this moment, and he could hardly believe they had changed so fast. He ascribed their hesitancy to prudence, to the caution that comes in alien surroundings.

"How far up to this reggae place?" said Caroline. "I'm getting tired."

She was tired? Fifteen minutes ago she had been dying to dance. For Raven that clinched it; Eric and Caroline did suspect him of harboring nasty intentions. He thought he should feel piqued by this, offended, but he felt a tickling gratification, levity over something not yet discovered. Were they the affluent prey he was seeking?

Drawn together by their alarm, Eric and Caroline had turned. They were both looking down the hill for an escape route, but to Raven they appeared disoriented. Beyond the canal and parallel to it was a rising street, and past that stood a stucco fence that formed one border of the residence's property. Raven could see a corner of the building, one of the cement balconies, the slanted green roof. To reach the entrance Eric and Caroline had merely to backtrack across the bridge and follow the street curving round to the front of the residence, but neither of them seemed to recognize anything. Without him, Raven thought, they would get lost, and because of this they were reluctant to leave him. He had them in his power for the night.

"We're almost there," he said, and as if oblivious to their anxiety, he pointed a finger at the hilltop. "That music is it."

It came from up in the darkness, a Jamaican voice supported by horns and drums, and Raven, ever the gregarious escort, assured Eric and Caroline that they would like the place. Walker's, as it was called, attracted the calm and the tolerant, and in addition, it possessed a panoramic view. They relented.

Soon the street had become level again and where it angled to the right, Caroline paused for breath. A hand to her chest, she denigrated her smoking habit, but then she rummaged through her bag for a cigarette and matches. Eric rolled his eyes at Raven, ironic maliciousness in his smile, and to show he was in superior shape, he started pumping his arms and legs like a man sprinting. If he intended to impress, he failed; Raven saw the exhibition as a ludicrous outpouring of machoism. Did these two have a sex life? What did they have in common? To judge by what they had said to him so far, they had very little in common, and going by externals, they had nothing. The yellow and blue in Caroline's blouse and jeans outfit contrasted entirely with Eric's black clothing. Eric wore no jewelry, not even a watch; but Caroline had on a crystal ring, an opal-colored wristlet, and the necklace of wooden beads. Few married pairs of elder years could have looked more dissimilar than they did, and as they all resumed their approach to Walker's, Caroline smoking, Eric humming, the sound of the music getting louder, Raven began to think about the product of this coupling, the daughter. What sort of personality did she have?

Now Raven could smell the marijuana and the walking room in the street had narrowed. Parked along its edges were cars and motorcycles, and the raggedly dressed guys collected on the hoods and fenders passed their joints from hand to hand. Voices were low, bodies relaxed, and expressions ranged from sleepy to pensive. In Walker's the record went on playing, the Jamaican star singing of Africa. Flanked by Eric and Caroline, Raven stepped onto a paved walk and although he did not see anyone move, he could sense that heads had swiveled. With his curly hair and his light brown skin, he was often taken for a Martinican, and he could almost hear the men saying that he must be a professional guide, someone these tourists had hired in order to visit interesting spots not shown on their maps.

Caroline tossed her cigarette into the darkness. Out on the dirt bordering the walk were prone forms, and a man with knobby braids stood by a bush urinating. The odor of the urine was intense, and even with the music going, Raven heard the clucking of a tongue and a mumbled curse, sharp disgust expressed by Eric. "They piss anywhere, these people. I've noticed that." The path became two cracked steps, a man with a scowl and a patchy beard nodded at Raven, and then he, Eric

51

and Caroline were inside Walker's, standing together near the entrance. "It's free to get in," said Raven, speaking loud to compete with the song, and the condition of the once private house revealed why this was so: scarred gray walls, cheap plank flooring, no windows, red bulbs shining weakly in the ceiling fixtures. Who would pay admission to this? Eric, rooted to the boards, shuddered, but Caroline got into sync with the music and her sinuous movements took her to the room where several men, but no women, were dancing. Raven went in and caught her by the arm. Insistent but polite, he turned her around and he motioned toward the flight of stairs that connected this floor to the upper one.

"It's better up above," he said. "Come on."

She fell in behind him with Eric following. Their weight on the stairs made the bannister shake. Down in the yard, visible from the stairs, the women in shifts and kerchiefs had their kitchen set up, the massive pots and pans, the portable grills over charcoal fires, and they were dishing out portions of stewed chicken, boiled yams, *dashin, accra.* They were talking incessantly, toddling about, serving the ones hungry after an hour or two of dancing, and their business tonight looked brisk. "Smells delicious," said Caroline. "Real local food." And she, Raven and Eric got to the second floor where marijuana vapors engulfed them again. It was warm and crowded but not stuffy. Two sides of the floor lay open to the air and bounded by a flimsy wooden balustrade, and in the dimness of the red lighting, the tips of the joints in the sucking mouths glowed like embers. Raven asked Eric and Caroline what they wanted to drink.

He moved to the bar and put his hands on the counter. The wood against his fingers was abrasive and unpolished. As he spoke to the woman with chestnut bangs, a Swiss woman with whom he had once flirted, he saw Caroline coming toward him, weaving through the men who canvassed her from behind. Her hand touched his shoulder, her breath blew against his neck. "Forget the beer. I'll have one later." And he looked back to see her entering the crammed dance area, one blonde head among the frizzy curls, the whiskered chins, the dreadlocks. "Make it 'deux biere,'" he said to the woman, and he gave her his money for the bottles, which she had uncapped.

He and Eric stood by one of the railings. The ice cold beer stung his throat but tasted pleasantly bitter. A new song with love as its theme had begun and in the alcove past the bar the man on the cushioned stool was leaning over a turntable, preparing the next record. Raven could see his red woolen hat, a bristly sideburn, the golden spangle in his earlobe. When he had the disc in position, the man pulled a cigarette from his pocket, and while he was smoking he gazed through the sheet of glass separating him from the dancers in the tile-floored room. Raven had a diagonal view of the room, and looking through the doorway frame he felt admiration for Caroline's spunk. Only one other woman had joined the men dancing, a younger girl in an olive shirt, her yellow-brown skin glossy with sweat, and nobody save Caroline was white. He had met tourists who thought that dreadlocks meant black hatred, black animosity, but she had plunged in among these guys as if contemptuous of such thinking. Planted in the space she had made for herself, she was letting her arms and hips go, and already she had her eyes half-closed; already and without the use of ganja she had fallen into the somnolent state that characterized these reggae enthusiasts.

He and Eric drank their beers, emptying the bottles.

"Time for some grass?" said Eric. "I'm in the mood."

"Me, too."

"You can get some?"

"If you give me the money."

Eric obliged, handing over the cash, and downstairs Raven went to the scowling man sitting on the steps before the entrance. Presented with the bills, one hundred francs' worth, the man floated off toward the street, and when he returned a minute later he had a small ziplock bag and a sheaf of rolling papers. "Tiens." Raven took the goods, satisfying himself with a quick feel of the ganja. "Jusquu la prochain," he said - until next time - and he found Eric gnawing on his thumbnail when he got back to him.

"My wife isn't tired anymore, is she?"

"She likes to dance."

"The cigarettes don't affect her now, do they?"

"I guess she's enjoying herself."

"Enjoying it with all those guys so close."

"Let's see if we can sit," said Raven.

Together they sidled through the standing groups, together they eyed the picnic tables aligned by the rear balustrade. The men on the benches sat dozing, sat smoking, sat lost in the music and their own contemplations, and Raven could read the melancholy etched in some of the faces. Through these faces he could discern a general longing to escape the world, a longing to find the kingdom of paradise. "Excuse me," he said, nudging a shoulder clad in fishnet fabric, and the man with his head and two stout arms resting heavy on the tabletop awoke from his dream of heaven, slid over on the bench so that Raven would have room beside him. Opposite Raven, trying sign language, Eric appealed to a rouge-faced woman filling the pipe she was sharing with her boyfriend, but since his gestures seemed to confuse her, Raven interceded with his French. They huddled over the table, Eric and Raven, and Raven slipped a few of the papers off the sheaf. He laid them flat, made the creases, sprinkled in the ganja. "You have the matches?" he asked Eric, and Eric delved into his wife's pocketbook, which he was holding so she could dance. Eric lit one of the five joints rolled, but when he inhaled his eyes watered. A tissue of smoke came out of his nostrils. He tried to keep the rest in his lungs, but at last they rebelled and he had to cough, the expulsion a cloud black as soot. Raven relieved him of the joint.

"Gotta get used to this again," said Eric. "It's been years since my L.A. days."

"That's where you used to live?"

"In Santa Monica. We had a hell of a life there. Great for awhile."

And as Raven took his turn with the ganja, as he felt it warming him, spreading through him, seeping into his bones and muscles, he saw the need to probe Eric for information. Every person had an Achilles heel and one had only to find it in the victim to exploit it. How could he put his acquaintance with Eric and Caroline to advantageous use? They could not be of value to him unless they had wealth, and he doubted they had any wealth staying as they were in the crummy residence.

"It isn't a palace," Eric said when Raven asked him why they had chosen it. "But what's so terrible. It's just for tonight and our daughter said it's the cheapest thing around. Why waste the bucks on an overpriced hotel?"

Eric grabbed the joint back and with each pull he struggled to hold the smoke. Raven encouraged him. In loosening Eric up, priming him for the innocuous questions, the ganja had become a tool for Raven, an ally, and it seemed completely normal that during their conversation Raven would ask Eric

54

what he did for a living.

"I'm semi-retired. Quit the rat race years ago."

"You don't look that old."

"Forty-seven. But I have the yoga and my jogging..."

The song on now was a militant hit sung by a man with a gruff voice. Eric snickered with his teeth bared and then said something in reference to his wife.

"What?" said Raven, whose mind had drifted, but Eric had the joint in his mouth again and was looking over the balustrade at their side. "You weren't kidding," he said. "Nice view." And Raven joined him in enjoying the vista, scanning the neighborhood below Walker's, the messy sprawl of cobbled lanes, tin and shingled roofs, garden plots, palm trees. Far to the left stood a high white wall encircling the tombs and crosses of a cemetery, and about half a mile in front of Walker's were the lights dotting the hill of Trenelle, another residential district.

"Just look at the sky," said Eric. "The number of stars you can see!"

He struck a match for their second joint and Raven watched him take a hit. Eric still had a film of water blurring his eyes.

"Forty-seven and semi-retired," Raven said. "That's an achievement."

"Don't I know it. I busted my tail when I was young. I started with nothing."

Too stoned for the pretense of modesty, Eric embarked on a proud discourse concerning himself. He described how he, a Brooklyn boy, a ghetto child, had endured a series of inane jobs to push himself through college; how with the speed of a corporate wizard he had climbed the ladder in his first company, a Wall Street brokerage firm; how in five or six years he had branched out on his own, started his own business, invested his profits wisely in stocks and bonds and real estate; how, his fortune made, he had gotten sick of the stress, the meetings, the secretary's buzzer, the starchy collars, the ties, the sycophantic employees and the morass of paperwork; how with Caroline's approval he had sold his business and many of his stocks and moved the family to California, Santa Monica, a seaside house for the sun and the ocean, the bliss of his semi-retirement. Freed from the bondage of a strict schedule, he had unwound into a life of bumming on the beach and surfing, his days enhanced by plenty of grass and a little cocaine and the sex nearly every morning and night with Caroline.

"And your daughter?" Raven asked.

"She loved it there. I'd get up, drive her to school, come back home and get into bed again with Caroline. We'd have breakfast - I cooked - and then I'd go to the beach while she did whatever she wanted to do. Usually I'd pick up Bianca and later I'd hit the beach again or take a drive along the coast. I used to love to drive."

"So what went wrong?"

"Nothing."

"But you left."

"We left. But that was because both me and Caroline missed New York."

And so there was Westchester, where they lived now, and their elegant house tucked into the woods in a suburban community. "I have my spiritual pursuits and a private teacher for it," Eric said. "Caroline calls him my guru, making fun, but the hell with her. For me it's real direction, inspiration, and I keep my hand in the business end just enough to keep my cash flow positive."

"Does Caroline work?"

"Are you kidding? She works at using her credit cards, that's all."

Eric relit the joint and took the rest of it for himself. Did he want another? Raven began to give him one, but his outthrust arm was ignored. "She can't still be dancing," Eric blurted, and his knuckles smacked against the table, drawing a glance from the girl with the pipe. He rose from the bench with his hand on the railing and his head pushed forward on his stringy neck, and as he stood glaring through the dimness he looked like a dog on the scent of an enemy. 'Americain,' said a voice. 'Sauvage.' But Eric had not heard the comment and Raven kept his laughter inside. The record going now was a reggae classic, a ballad of yearning, and the tautness in Eric's rope-thin body showed he was deaf to the music, too. He said he had to find his wife, see what in hell she was doing, but Raven, anxious to keep him at the table, did the job for him, walking to the edge of the dance room floor and peering across it. Hemmed in a corner and hugging herself, Caroline remained a striking sight among the grubby rastas, and although some of them had her under surveillance, she herself seemed rapt in a dream, a vision suited to the mood of the song. Her face, lifted toward the ceiling, had sadness in it, and the sheen of moisture under her eyes could as easily have been from tears as from sweat. Raven was shocked. But when he rejoined Eric at the table he put a lid on his amazement, reporting with all due nonchalance that Caroline had yet to slow down.

"She doesn't have a partner?"

"You don't need one for this kind of music."

"But she has one."

"No. She doesn't."

As a distraction, Raven handed Eric another joint. Like candy for a child, it pacified him, and Raven resisted the lulling desire to withdraw into his own thoughts and let his mind soar on the wings of the ganja. After a suitable interval of silence, he mentioned Eric's daughter, Bianca, and he pointed out that few Americans lived in Martinique. Why had she chosen to come here when there were all the English-speaking islands in the Caribbean?

"French. She wanted to learn French."

"But not in France."

"She loves hot weather. Maybe she got that from California."

Through his questioning, subtle but persistent, Raven discovered that Eric and Caroline had been visiting their daughter for the past week. They had rented a car so Bianca could show them around and each evening they had returned to her Fort de France apartment. This afternoon, however, Bianca had left the island, going with some others on a chartered yacht sailing to the Grenadines, and instead of dealing with copied keys or the trusting of her keys to a neighbor in the building, Eric and Caroline had packed their valises and checked into the residence. As Eric had said, they were staying there for just one night, and early in the morning they would hire a cab to take them to the airport.

"It's four or five days sailing through the Grenadines," Eric said.

"Can't be bad."

"Oh, she loves it. Bianca loves to be on boats."

Two thick arms enwrapped Eric's chest from behind, an opal wristlet clasped on one of them. The crystal ring on Caroline's hand snagged against her husband's shirt, silver twinkling in the black folds. Caroline laid her chin on Eric's shoulder and to Raven it was clear that she had wiped the distress from her face. "Is it good?" she said, and pursed her lips in an indication that she wanted to sample the ganja. Eric reached up and put the joint in her mouth, holding it for her while she inhaled, yet in no other way did he respond to her sudden warmth. He became taut again, like a frozen rope, and when she kissed him on the neck he clucked his tongue with annoyance.

"We were just talking about Bianca," he told his wife.

Straddling the bench, her back to the railing, Caroline squeezed in beside him. They all smoked some of the joint and Raven listened to the gush of parental blather. Eric and Caroline spared him the wallet photo, but they said their daughter was pretty, said that with her habitual swimming she had sloughed off her baby fat. She was smart (in school she had been a terrific student), and she had a winning personality (when she was at home the phone always rang for her), and what sort of girl but a girl with grit would come to an island where she knew no one and would have to learn the language used? That was Bianca, their Bianca. She loved to explore and she had no qualms about being alone in a foreign environment.

"You'll have to give me her address," said Raven. "I'll look her up."

"She'd like that," Eric said. "I'm sure she would."

Raven had heard what he needed to know, but once started on the subject of their daughter, Eric and Caroline would not stop. This couple that bickered so much treasured their only child, and as Raven saw it, they could have no worse fear than losing her. He tried to imagine Bianca and how, in southern California, they had raised her, and he could not but see a spoiled individual, a girl who had never lacked for comfort.

And didn't I once live in a castle? Didn't I once live like a prince? But my princess belonged to a family of monsters and my inheritance would have been slaving for the beasts. Nice to have parents, isn't it girl? Nice to be abroad knowing you have that home sweet home to return to. But don't take pity on me. I'm surviving. And your parents..they'll pay what I ask to save your life.

Out on the road sloping down toward the canal, the ferocious barking of the scavenger dogs quieted Eric and Caroline. They walked faster, leery of the garbage pickers, and Raven matched his steps to theirs, his hands buried in his pockets. He thought the kidnapping could succeed, but to do it he would have to find a partner. Would Larry go for the plan?

Larry detested New York City and the money he could get as a ransom would permit him to quit his job and vacate his Bronx apartment. But before anything else was done, Larry would have to watch Eric and Caroline, gather information on them, verify that they had the wealth Eric claimed they did. There would be no reason to snatch Bianca if her parents were less than well-to-do.

In the residence hallway, outside their door, Caroline wrote Bianca's address on a scrap of lined paper, and underneath that she scribbled the address and the telephone number of their family's house. Anytime he wanted, whenever he got back to the States, Raven could come visit them in Westchester.

"We'd love to have you," Caroline said, and Eric gave him the bag of ganja and the three leftover joints.

"Have a good night," Raven said.

"You have a good year."

Raven sat at the table in his room and began writing his letter to Larry: 'We'll put them through some terror. We'll put this little family to the test.'

Chapter Eight

They were back home in Westchester and she had her room and he had his. The two doors opened onto the opposite ends of the long upstairs hall. Since their return the springtime weather had been mild and dry, ideal for tennis, but Caroline was sorry to have lost her tan and regretted having flown straight home with Eric. Unlike Eric she could speak Spanish and from Martinique she would have enjoyed going to Puerto Rico, though anything she might have said about wanting to travel by herself would have prompted an argument from him. And he, to her unending irritation, controlled the purse strings. There were times when she would wake up at night criticizing herself, chastizing herself for having become a prisoner in a gilded cage. They lived in their regal house surrounded by an acre of woods, she had her car and the wallet full of credit cards, and every year she renewed her membership in the country club where she played tennis. Out on the courts and in the jacuzzi, in the sauna and at the side of the swimming pool, she had made herself some friends, mainly among the other idle wives, and this group of women would often take the commuter train to Manhattan. For a night or two they would sleep in the city, at the Plaza Hotel, and they would dine like royalty, go to the theater, shop. They would stand for fittings and discuss the clothing styles. In her closets, Caroline had a huge assortment of clothes, but fashions were fashions and in her group you had to keep up. She did keep up, buying even the smartest riding apparel for her horseback jaunts from the local stable. But underneath the finery, at her core, she could feel an emptiness, could admit to herself that her life was hollow. She had never held a job or acquired a professional skill, and she blamed nobody as she blamed herself for this uselessness, this dependence, her subordination to her husband's money.

When he had been working in New York, she had been busy caring for Bianca, a child then, and when they had moved to California and he had begun his semi-retirement, she had been happy simply with their new locale and all the time they got to spend together. Even in those days she had occupied herself with country club diversions; she had gone on the shopping sprees that added bulk to her wardrobes. But none of this had seemed humdrum yet, none of it empty, perhaps because of the richness at her center, the harmony in the house. Between herself and Eric everything had been in balance. They'd had domestic calm, their mutual desire, and the joy of seeing Bianca excel in school. Those had been the days of the long sunny mornings she and Eric passed in bed, and content with this life, wanting nothing more than this life, she had watched the California years go by without giving much thought to the future. Then, desirous for another change of scenery, she and Eric had come back east, Bianca with them, and she had expected things to continue more or less as they had been. In this she was wrong. The fights between Bianca and her had started, and on a visit to the Bronx Botanical Gardens Eric had met the man she despised, his guru.

Ashok was his name, or what he called himself. He spoke English with a clipped Indian accent and said he had been born in Calcutta. "I'm a fakir," he told Caroline when Eric introduced him to her at the house. But the way he comported himself, grinning whenever he answered a question, lowering his eyes whenever he spoke at length, made her think of a different word, the word 'faker.' On this occasion he wore a checked tie and a blue flannel suit, but his pants and jacket were so scraggly that Caroline was sure he was bent on cultivating an image, on living up to a western idea of the eastern sage unconcerned with his worldly appearance. She found it unbelievable that her husband, successful in business and never a dupe, put himself under the guru's influence. Eric had not been raised by religious parents, nor had he ever mentioned having the wish to adopt a faith or pursue a spiritual path. And yet, after the years of work and the years of leisurely living in California, the alternative offered by the guru must have met an inner need. He hired Ashok as his personal teacher and embraced the program of discipline he was given. At Eric's request, Ashok and his midget assistant installed themselves in a specially built shack on the property, and at their command, true to his pledge of sexual abstinence, he converted the guest bedroom into his own sleeping quarters. But Caroline still had her appetites. What did he expect her to do? Her endearments ignored, her caresses shrugged off, Caroline became indignant, and she scoffed when he said that she should join him under Ashok's tutelage.

"We could do this together," he said.

"Waste your own time, not mine."

To satisfy her body she had to seduce other men. At first she felt uncomfortable doing this, but after a few infidelities the affairs were a part of her routine. Having lost none of her love for Eric, she urged patience on herself, and she made up her mind to stick by him, to wait until he had gone through his mystic phase. But the months went by. And Eric, despite her forbearance, kept causing problems; he took her lusty cruising more seriously than she did. Although neglectful of her sensual wants, he would throw tantrums when she arrived home from her nights out, and this behavior, irrational and egoistic, she refused to accept with good grace. She began to taunt Eric, began reporting the details of her adventures, and from that time on the bitterness between them had deepened. Now they had become addicted to quarreling, their clashes a daily occurrence. But Caroline was weary of their jawing, saw the absurdity of it, and she had discarded the notion that Eric was going through a mere phase. Absorbed by his soul-expanding program, he continued to swear by Ashok as his mentor. And she had decided to sue for divorce, leave the area, battle for a just settlement and take her chances on her own.

*****

Caroline was playing tennis with one of her friends, a woman who taught math at the local public high school. Every Saturday morning they had their singles game and during the warm-up Caroline would adjust to the school's hard courts, a challenge after a week of hitting on the country club's slow clay courts. Of comparable skill and ability, Caroline and her friend had fought through hundreds of close matches over the years and this morning, with each of them in sharp form, they had split two sets. Caroline suggested they play the third, the rubber set, though she, winded by their long rallies, had lost the second one. Her friend held this advantage: as a non-smoker she had better endurance than Caroline did. But Caroline hated going home without having reached a definite resolution, a victory or a loss, and today, in the cool weather, she felt that she could recover her strength and beat her friend. By the metal post at one end of the net she sipped the salty mineral water in her thermos bottle, devoured the quartered orange she had been holding in her sports bag. Helped by the liquid and fruit combination, she felt revived when she went onto the court again, and crouching low at the baseline she readied herself to receive serve.

This point she won, her forehand return untouchable. But after that, employing an arsenal of lobs and spins, her friend sucked her into the extended rallies, the stamina duels, and Caroline dropped six games in a row. Angry with herself, she picked up a ball and gave it a savage swipe with her racquet. It flew over three occupied courts and the high iron fence beyond them. In the parking lot it rolled to a rest between the front tires of her car. At the back of the car, a red Corvette, there rose a youngish-looking man dressed in dull colors, and Caroline had a suspicion (she didn't know why) that he had just broken into her trunk. "In the middle of the morning?" she said. "With people around?" She would have shouted at this violation, but the man, too far away to see in detail, appeared to be empty-handed. And as he left, strolling out of view behind a concrete slab, a wing of the school, she was distracted by the voice of her friend, talking about the match they had played.

"Don't gloat," Caroline said.

"Who's gloating? I happened to be on that set and you weren't."

"Have a good week."

The trunk had not been busted open, the windows were whole, nowhere on the car did she find evidence of vandalism. She threw her athletic bag onto the passenger seat, and strapped into the black harness, the safety belt, she put the key in the ignition. From the package on the dash she lifted out a cigarette, and she waited for the click of the steel coil, the automatic lighter, to get it lit. In the wake of her loss the acrid taste of the nicotine was something she welcomed, but a fleck of tobacco got into her windpipe and provoked a spell of coughing. Half-done with the cigarette, she crushed it out in the sliding dish. She used her thumb to rub some ashes off her nails. Caroline realized that her collapse in the tennis game had been due to her smoking habit, but one reason she smoked, or smoked as much as she did, was because of the discontent gnawing at her mind. It would be a struggle to give up cigarettes, but she made a vow to start trying on the first day of the new era, the day she would file for the divorce.

Caroline spun the radio dial until she found a rock music station. Electric guitars scratched and twanged as a woman's voice told a macabre story. Bothered by the sun streaks on the windshield, Caroline pawed through her bag for her tinted glasses, and when she came to a traffic signal, a red light, she stared at herself in the rearview mirror. The blackframed shades, hiding wrinkles, gave her a youthful look and that was without any cosmetics. But were the scars of age, the puckers and ridges, beginning to take her over? She thought not, she thought she had aged well, and her ongoing success as a sexual cruiser bore her out. Apart from the dye in her blonde coif she preserved herself through natural means, the tennis, the swimming at the club, and with her wide cheekbones and milk-clear skin, she was confident her allure would last for years. She could not reproach Bianca for thinking of her with envy. Bianca had inherited Eric's bland countenance and coming from her daughter, envy of her physical attributes was like a compliment.

Behind Caroline a horn squealed, alerting her to the green light. "Move it, lady! Are you blind?" In her sideview mirror she saw a face, the irate face of a bull-necked man with his head slanting out his window, and from the rest of the cars held up in her lane she heard a chorus of beeping protests. "Fuck you all," she said quietly, and she turned the Corvette onto a street lined with private houses. Every yard had its boundary of hedges, every lawn had its shrubs, and in the manicured neatness of the neighborhood, Caroline felt as if she were driving through some vast topiary maze, a green labyrinth studded with buildings where the captive people took their shelter, beguiled themselves with their toys. And they were so enchanted with these toys they did not even think of themselves as confined. Was this her world, the world where she belonged? Up till recently she would have said yes, but none of it had ever seemed so geometric, so measured, so imprisoning in its orderliness.

Guitars shrieking, discord triumphant, the song on the radio was reaching its climax. Caroline footpumped the gas until the speedometer touched sixty. She wanted to get into the country, to spend the afternoon away from Eric and this area. But something had come unstuck on the Corvette, and now the tail section was bumping up and down, wobbling despite her grip on the wheel. Fearful of an accident, she pressed her foot against the brake. She heard a raspy noise like metal dragging against the cement. "No," she said. "Not this morning." But she knew it was there, a flat tire, and when she had pulled the car over, stepping outside to inspect the damage, she cursed the vandal from the tennis courts. Had he done this only to her car? Had he done it because it was a red Corvette, a sporty machine that he coveted? Whatever his motivation, he had cut a gash in her back left tire, and the hoop of rubber sat frayed and useless around the chromium hubcap.

Off went the radio, off the engine. She raised the moldy blanket in her trunk and found the spare in usable condition. After lifting it out, she put it next to the flat and she armed herself with the tools at her disposal: a jack, a crowbar and a monkey wrench. "Go to it, girl," she admonished herself. "Do the job." Yet she did nothing but stand like an idiot, puzzling over the replacement procedure. And it would be too pathetic, too embarrassing, to knock on somebody's door asking for help in changing the tire. Caroline dropped the tools beside the spare and at a loss over how to proceed, she leaned against the Corvette pouting. Dirt and grease had got onto her white short-sleeved sweater and she noticed particles of rust under her fingernails, under the red polish.

From behind her in the road a car went by, swerving into the opposite lane for clearance. Caroline felt the wind from its passing and like one forlorn, one stranded on an island while a ship sails by near the shore, she watched it going away from her, a compact model getting smaller every second. A feeling of pure helplessness made her kick the flat tire, rest her head on the Corvette's roof, but when she looked up again that car, the beige compact, was coming in her direction. Its sole occupant was the driver, and beneath the lowered sun flap she could see a spike of red hair. Hopeful but wary, ready for the worst, Caroline picked up the crowbar and in the gravel dip across the road the wheels came crunching to a stop. The glass in the window slid down. "Having trouble?" The voice was friendly but not pushy, the eyes held intelligence and reserve, and the crookedness in the facial bones, the asymmetry of the features, hinted at a past disfigurement.

"The tire's slit," Caroline said.

"You need help?"

"I can't ask you to change it."

"I'm offering to."

His white tennis sneakers had frazzled laces and his blue and white sweatsuit, ankle-length pants with a mangy jacket, would have been demeaning for a beggar to wear. No fashion expert here, Caroline thought, no one likely to win an award for handsomeness, but in the briskness of his walk he projected the casual vigor, the nimble muscularity, of an athlete.

"I saw you playing before," he said. "You were at the tennis courts."

"I just finished. Some little piss-ass did this to me."

"I think I saw him. I should've said something."

He squatted by the tire and rigged the jack to the underside of the car. Trusting him to help her, Caroline relinquished the iron rod and this he used as his lever, hoisting part of the Corvette off the ground. Another vehicle approached, sleek as an arrow, and Caroline waved it on.

"This is too kind of you."

"Nothing to it."

The jack firm, the car stable, he pried off the hubcap with the rod. The chromium clanged against the cement. On one of the bolts he got the wrench fixed to the width he needed, and Caroline watched him jerking the tool, scraping the rust, loosening the cylindrical pin with repeated turns of his wrist. She took all the bolts as he unscrewed them and each time he put one into her cupped palm she noted the caution in his manner, the basic shyness that was there. At the slightest touch of her skin, the most insignificant grazing of their hand, he would withdraw his arm swiftly.

"I haven't even asked you your name," she said.

"Larry."

"Mine's Caroline."

Larry removed the dead piece of rubber. He balanced the spare up on the axle and aligned the holes for the reinsertion of the bolts. As Caroline gave them back to him his expression remained neutral, and nothing she said, none of her praise for his efficiency, evoked a ripple of acknowledgement. He slapped on the hubcap when the job was complete, he jacked the wheel down to the pavement, and although Caroline protested, insisting that he had done enough, more than enough, he scooped up the wrecked tire for her and dumped it into the trunk. Caroline threw in the tools and shut the hood.

"I have to learn how to change flats myself," she said.

"It's easy. But can I give you some advice?"

"Sure."

"It's about tennis. I think you can improve your forehand."

"My forehand? How do you know?"

"I watched you playing. You have a habit of jamming yourself."

"You must've been watching closely," Caroline said.

"Not that closely. It's an obvious thing you're doing."

"What a saint. He changes my tire and gives me a tennis tip."

"I really stopped to give you the tip. I could see how mad you were when you lost."

Caroline smirked, then broke out laughing. She asked him whether she could buy him lunch. Nearby, she said, there was an Italian restaurant that served a delicious spinach lasagna, and after they had the meal, after they digested the food, they could, if he had the time, drive back to the high school tennis courts. By hitting with her - and she would consider this another favor - he could assess her game more accurately. He could show her what she had to do to correct the technical faults in her strokes.

"I was planning on getting back to the city."

"You live in the city?"

"In the Bronx. I was up here today to practice with a friend."

But when his eyes, sparkling with their intelligence, began to evaluate her from the legs up, from the bottom of her white skirt up, when his mouth, until now rigidly prim, began to soften into a hesitant smile, Caroline felt with the certitude of knowledge that he would be following her in his car, a hungry dog on her leash. His desire was emboldening him, encouraging him in this modest impudence, and somehow she knew that he lived by himself, weighted with loneliness. And what had happened to put the tilt, the subtle disarrangement of bone, into his face? Had there been a trauma, a period of anguish and physical suffering? Even smiling his was a face imprinted with severity, and Caroline wanted to put him on the couch and make herself his psychoanalyst.

He crossed the road to get into his car. The developed shoulders, the tapering hips, the athleticism in his walk - his charms were there despite the disservice of the horrendous sweatsuit, and that could be shed for finer clothes. *You help me with my tennis and I'll teach you how to dress.* Caroline licked her pinky.

*****

Leaning out her bedroom window, Caroline looked up at

the geese in the sky. They were returning from their southern migrations and in the dark-shaded blue of the early evening, the flocks resembled scudding clouds. During the next several weeks they would keep coming in honking waves, and the geese who had these woods as their territory would land in the ponds near the house. Obedient to instinct, they would renew their acquaintance with the property unless they retained in the genius of their cells a memory of the previous summer, when Ashok and his midget assistant, with their taste for bird flesh, had hunted their numbers with high-powered rifles. The two supposed mystics had reduced the population she like feeding with bread crumbs, and even her husband, a yearly contributor to wildlife organizations, had spoken to Ashok in stringent tones he otherwise never used with the guru. "Stop killing them, or at least cut down," he said, and his spiritual guides agreed to shoot fewer birds, though they stated, in justification of their hunting, that they cooked whatever they shot. "You feed us well," they told Eric, but for both of them the height of gastronomic joy was the eating of a freshly killed fowl, a succulent goose or duck or pheasant. Equipped with their rifles, they would hunt when the impulse seized them, and they would dine on the grass behind their shack, roasting the birds on a spit over logs.

Caroline walked away from the window. She heard the tinkling of the dinner bell, rung downstairs by the midget, and from the other end of the hall came the creaking of the hinges on her husband's door. There was the sound of his feet in the nylon slippers coming toward her room, the assault of his knuckles against the mahogany wood that had stopped him. "You don't have to lock yourself in," he said. "You can join us at the table and Ashok won't mind." Caroline yawned, exaggerating the loudness of that noise, and through a torrent of invective, she made him know he had woken her up, ruined her rest. "Pardon me," Eric said. "Don't want to disturb the queen." A final blow from his hand or foot jarred the door and Caroline heard the rustle of his pants as he hurried toward the stairs.

She felt jubilant. Until last night she and Larry had met in the Bronx, inside his apartment, or at a motel close to the city. But then, during one of their tennis games, she had been inspired by the thought of risking a confrontation with Eric. She had imagined the thrill of having sex under her husband's nose and she told Larry they could do it in the bed where she and Eric had slept for years. "I'll be there," he said, and faithful to his promise, he arrived at two in the morning, whistling under her window. To one leg of her dresser she had fastened a sturdy rope, and when she threw it down to the yard, Larry put on his rubber gloves and began the climb. The moon was a yellow sickle. Out in the woods, in their hut, Ashok and the midget were asleep on the quilts they used as bedding, and despite the crispness of the air the night smelled of blossoming flowers. Could Larry do it? Did he have the strength in his arms? Up he came with the aid of his gloves and wearing the solid black clothes of a burglar, and at the ledge, impressed by his speed, dazzled by the absence of strain on his face, Caroline undid the clasps on her robe so that he could see her breasts in the moonlight. "Be there soon, fair maiden." And when he had reached the window, when he had crawled through the opening, Larry closed his mouth over one of her nipples, licking the areola. The climb had been unnecessary (she could have let him in by the front entrance), but that was what made its accomplishment erotic. Like foreplay, it had roused their juices for the main event, and after Caroline had pulled up the rope, they hastened to the bed and the sheets of cambric.

"This is where you two used to sleep?"

"Until he started following the guru."

"And now? Is he down the hall?"

"Last time I looked. Sleeping like a baby."

From the foot of the bed and above the honks of the passing geese, Caroline heard Eric calling. He still wanted her to come eat dinner, to sit with him, Ashok and the midget. Going by what she could smell of the food, Caroline guessed the midget had roasted a chicken (bought at the supermarket), and as a matter of fact, she was feeling the peptic stirrings of hunger. Yet to dine with those three, to listen to their talk of dharma, to endure their discussions on the kundalina fire, would give her indigestion. She would enjoy nothing at the table, and this even though the midget could cook. Caroline sighed. Because the midget liked to cook when Ashok gave him the time for it, because he spent a great many hours at the oven or the stove - the shack for him and Ashok had no cooking apparatus - she was now an outcast from her kitchen, venturing into it only when she knew she would be alone there.

"You can stop, Eric. She isn't coming."

With the words from Ashok, her husband went silent, and

Caroline sank back into her reverie. No more geese were in the sky, against the blue that was fading to black the moon had emerged as a silver horn, and as she lay amid her sheets, arms outflung and her head on the pillows, Caroline breathed the odor of Larry, deriving from this lingering scent the brief sensation of receiving one of his orgasms. Legs stretched over the end of the mattress, her satin robe drawn up into the V of her thighs, Caroline saw him as he became during those seconds of transport; he would go stiff but oddly quiet (even in the motel or his apartment), and his eyes would gleam with something akin to thankful wonder. Until meeting her, he had said, the women he had gone to for intimacy were prostitutes.

"It looks like a fabulous chicken."

This was Eric flattering the midget, Eric shouting so she could hear.

"I can't wait to dig in."

Before Larry's departure last night they had crept down to the kitchen naked, and on the enamel counter by the sink, Caroline had fixed them salami sandwiches. They had eaten while sitting on the high stools, and afterwards, a lit candle in her hand, Caroline had led her guest on a promenade through the house. "This Greek vase comes from a potter in Monterrey. The abstract painting above the chaise lounge I got from a Soho gallery."

"Marvelous," Larry had said, with derision. "Fucking marvelous." And as they moved from room to room, sliding their feet over waxed mahogany and Persian shag, they'd exchanged drolleries about her talent as an interior designer, the whole tour done for the satisfaction of walking nude while Eric slept.

Down in the dining room the midget was chanting. He was intoning his blessing over the dinner. For this he would be standing on the table, standing amidst the plates, glasses, napkins, and utensils, and Eric and Ashok would be in their chairs, hands folded, heads bowed. 'Mnnggmnnnnggg.' The midget's chant was a nasal vocalization, a pushing of wordless notes through the nostrils, and although it would last for just one minute, he had the capacity to do it for hours, having learned esoteric breathing techniques from monks who sang in the east.

I'm a stranger in my own house, Caroline thought, and with the idea of calling Larry she looked across the bed to her phone.

Would that help, a chat with Larry? It might, but only because Larry would let her gabble on for as long as she wanted. Unlike most of the men she knew, Larry could listen to someone other than himself. He was her confidant, her corporeal angel. At his urging, trying to break her habit, she had cut the amount of cigarettes she smoked by half, and under his informal coaching she had revamped her forehand and become a consistent winner against her teacher friend. Naturally, she had gotten him to peel his shell of shyness with her and she had prevailed upon Larry to chuck his ugliest clothes and wear the presentable things she had bought him. Progress on every front, it seemed, but in one respect they were stalled. Whenever she asked him to open up about himself, Larry reverted to reticence. For some unaccountable reason he turned remote. At best he would allude to his youth and an accident, a car crash that had been the cause of his facial reconstruction, and the most he would say about his family is that his parents were dead and he had a brother living in Oregon.

After a rise in pitch, the midget's chanting stopped. The cuckoo clock in the dining room warbled the hour, seven p.m. Caroline felt the evening's wind blowing through her curtains and she reached down between her thighs to unbunch her robe and cover her legs. She would go eat at a restaurant, she decided, but then the telephone was ringing, the line she had to herself, and she rolled across the bed groping for the table cluttered with magazines.

"Caroline?"

"Hey, Larry. I was just thinking about you."

"What's doing there?"

"They're eating. The three idiots."

"Can you get out?"

"I can do what I want. You should know that."

"Can you drive in?"

"What's wrong? It sounds like something's wrong."

"No. Nothing wrong. But there's something I have to tell you. I have to tell you in person, not over the phone." His voice weakened, clotted, grew slurred and incomprehensible.

"I can't understand you, Larry."

"Can't what? Oh, it's just that…it hurt tonight so I took some codeine. Had to."

"Take a nap then and I'll come in."

"Good. It's very important, what I have to tell you."

71

Larry hung up and the lively talk of two young women came through her receiver. 'It hurt tonight so I took some codeine. Had to.' Okay, she believed him; she had seen him in the clutches of the pain wrought by the nerve tissue in his face, the tissue that would be forever damaged by that mishap from his past. But after all the years of using the drug as a medication, of relying on it when the twinges struck, had he developed an addiction to it? Could he function properly without it?

An hour later she left her room, walked down the steps, and sashayed by the dining table in her calfskin boots. Eric, Ashok and the midget were drinking tea out of porcelain cups and Caroline went by slowly to give them a look at her black leather jacket and tight blue jeans. To mock their grim disapproval, she blew them all a sardonic kiss and at the door she bowed grandly. "It's like living with the Inquisition," she said, and with that parting shot she ambled off toward the driveway.

*****

On Larry's street in the Bronx the lamp posts lacked bulbs and every inch of pavement needed a scrubbing. Caroline parked her red Corvette as close to his building as she could, and as she strode up the block, she felt her boots grinding over splintered glass. She heard sirens in the distance and from somewhere near she could smell kerosene and burning rubber. Would her Corvette, which had no alarm, remain untouched one more time in this infernal zone? Through the entranceway of a pizzeria, a man proclaimed his want for her - "Stop, baby. Where you goin'?" - and down at the corner two men wearing baseball caps were cursing each other out in Spanish.

Larry can stomach living here, can do no better than this for a home?

Twice she rang the button by his name and the glass door off the foyer buzzed. She pushed it roughly and went through, quickened her walk to catch the elevator. Inside the graffitied car stood an older man with the stink of alcohol on him, and even before they had begun to ascend, his liquor-smudged eyes were staring at her, sizing her up, drilling into her skin with racial hostility. One, two, three, four...the numbers in the panel lit up as they rose, and this black tenant seemed about to ask what a woman like her, a white woman of obvious breeding, was doing in the ghetto after dark.

"You goin' to see my man Larry?"

The elevator had stopped at six and Caroline turned left in

the dim passage. Spinning her head, she looked over her shoulder, and she saw the black thumb press the edge of the door to hold it open.

"If you're seein' Larry, tell him Bugs has a tip. Heavenly Angel in the first tomorrow at Belmont. Can't miss."

Something that had been alive, perhaps a pet dog or cat, was sending a vile stench up through the incinerator chute, and on the drab walls of the passage were smutty witticisms and lewd drawings. A person could eavesdrop on the apartments by listening through the doors, and as Caroline advanced toward Larry's she heard the weeping of an infant, voices raised in family conflict, the talking coming from the televisions. And none of these sounds diminished one jot when she stepped into Larry's; it seemed as if nothing any thicker than cardboard divided the flats in this tenement.

He has changed in appreciable ways, Caroline thought, for when she had first visited him each of his rooms had been like a pigsty. Socks and shirts lying everywhere, the bathroom sink too off-putting for her to use, a cake of grease and crust on the stove and the spillage of crumbs in the nook of a kitchen allowing the roaches to thrive; no bachelor could have improved on the messiness, the indifference to disorder, and no explanation from his mouth could have summed up in plainer terms just how lonely a life he led. That he had apologized for the apartment, that he had cleaned it quite thoroughly and kept it tidy ever since, was heartening proof that she had made an impact on him, a mark however minor.

"What did you want to tell me?" she asked.

She was sitting at the table in the front room toying with the dice from his backgammon board, and she watched him run the water in the kitchen. He splashed it over his face and neck to rouse himself from his codeine nod, and on a whim, because she knew he disliked it, she lit a cigarette from the pack in her bag.

"And don't tell me it was a ruse. A trick to get me to come over. You were serious on the phone. There's something you need to get off your chest."

Larry had on white tennis shorts, nothing else, and Caroline blew out ovals of smoke looking at him. Nineteen years her junior, he was, with regard to his body, a treat, and she should have been glad to have him as her candy. But why this evasive mode of his? Why the enigmatic silences?

"Whatever you're bottling up let go."

He twisted the faucet taps to shut them, but through inattention he left the water dripping. As he moved past the table, he ran his knuckles against her cheek, and from across the room he smiled at her with a troubled air, an attitude of guilt. "What is it, Larry? What are you afraid of me knowing?" But he had taken his eyes off her, was stooping amidst the weight-lifting equipment on the floor.

"You'd have laughed if you'd seen me awhile ago," he said. "I was like a skeleton."

He chose a dumbbell, stood, began doing curls with his right arm. With each curl his bicep bulged and relaxed. Caroline flung her cigarette into the kitchen sink, and as his workout went on, she felt sadder and sadder. For someone who had brains as well as physical vitality, Larry seemed a gross underachiever, and she could not comprehend why he made no attempt to leave this apartment, this ravaged area of the Bronx.

"Just how much do you gamble?" she said.

"What?"

"The backgammon, the horse racing. Is this a compulsion with you?"

"No. Where'd that idea come from?"

He gambled, he had a mania for tennis, and here in this hole he eked out his existence, finding relief from old wounds in the codeine. Scanty facts, what she knew of him, but she had grown tired of trying to dig through his defenses and into his psyche.

"Heavenly Angel in the first tomorrow at Belmont. Your friend said that in the elevator."

"Bugs? You ran into Bugs?"

"He said it can't miss."

"Thanks for the message."

"Don't mention it. And when you're willing to talk, really talk, give me a ring."

She had gone out into the hall, closing the door behind herself, when she heard the crash of the dumbbell. And after that Larry was speaking, as if to inform a secret associate that he was caught in a dilemma: "Raven, what now? It's you or her, and either way I'll feel like a piece of shit."

Chapter Nine

Charles opened his eyes smelling ammonia. Pain flared inside his head, a pain that rolled through his skull like fire, and above him he saw the glowering face of Raven. In Raven's hand was a bottle of the all-purpose cleaner that he, Charles, kept on board the boat. "Awake?" said Raven. "Awake now?" and Raven put the cap on the container, sealing the source of the fumes. Careful not to scratch himself, Charles rubbed the top of his head with one finger, and through his hair, the thick pad of curls, he felt a bump and raw stickiness. Though still woozy, he began to sit up, and without remembering much at first, he gazed at the wreckage in the cabin. Around him on the floor, dented and chipped, lay his precious video cassettes, the tapes he had spent years collecting. It looked as if most of them had been ruined, and the video machine, bolted to the shelf along with his color TV, had been smashed to pieces.

"What the hell happened?" Raven said. "Who did this?"

Charles got up, shaky on his feet, and kicked at the piles of destroyed cassettes. So many times he had watched these films, immersed himself in these fantasy worlds of erotica. And until Danielle had come, discovering his collection, going beserk over it, this roomy cabin had been his private refuge. Actually, he had considered the whole yacht his refuge; he had thought of it as the one place he could go when he felt the need to escape everything. More than a luxury possession, the boat was a central part of his life, and when he was alone on it, sailing or just tied up to the dock, he could forget the house, his parents, the business and even Danielle. He had nothing but love for *The Lucky Blonde*.

"It was my sister," he told Raven. "A completely unexpected visit."

"Danielle? What was she doing out so late?"

"She said she had to see me."

"God. And she hit you with that?" Raven pointed at the short metal pipe lying amid the mess on the floor.

"With that," said Charles. "She saw it by the sink and wham...I was out."

"You're lucky you woke up at all."

Eager for air, Charles walked up the steps to the deck. Over the wharf and across the bay, past all the other stationary boats, the horizon was aglow with stars. They were like beacons, invitations to set his sails and never come back. But how could he leave Martinique knowing Danielle needed him here? How could he desert his sister and still manage to live with himself? Left to the mercy of their parents and the doctors, she would feel that she had no allies in the world, and the loneliness that would inevitably follow, the desperation, might very well lead her to commit suicide. He would not want to have that on his conscience.

"I have to go," he called down to Raven. "I have to see if she went home."

"You think she did?"

"I hope so. She could be wandering around the streets in a daze."

At the waterfront bar, the Abracotier, a pianist was playing sentimental music for a French singer. Among the patrons at the outdoor tables Charles could see people he knew, people who kept their own yachts moored to this same dock. They had come to Martinique from Europe, most of them, and on the island they and their like formed an unorthodox set, a clique of sea-going, world-travelling bums. Young bums, too, Charles thought, while he at his age, 31, had already slipped into a rut. Between his sister and the business he had all kinds of responsibilities, and he envied the nomads for their vagabondage, envied them for having broken with the obligations from their pasts.

"You're making a mistake," said Raven, who had climbed up from down below and joined him at the stern. "You're doing something I have to pity."

"What's that?"

"Letting your family run your life. Danielle and her problems. I know that you love her, but you shouldn't live your whole life for her benefit."

Amazed at how well Raven had read him, Charles studied his face by the light coming from the bar. In the depths of the eyes, the blackish pools, he saw malignance wedded to cunning, and in the coarse-lipped mouth he perceived a ruthlessness that Raven's smile could not camouflage. What was going on in Raven's mind? he wondered. Why did he suspect that Raven wanted to involve him in something criminal? Once, when exceedingly drunk, Raven had told him that he was a fugitive from the forces of American law, but Charles had not been able to learn what he'd done. Murder? Drug dealing? A sexual assault? In essence Raven was a mystery to him, a dark puzzle, but Charles enjoyed it whenever they met. Their talks gave him the opportunity to use his English, to sharpen his English grammar and increase his vocabulary. He had studied English during his years in school and had spent some time doing real estate business in Florida.

Charles said, "You think I should leave, go away, and tough luck for my sister?"

"To put it brutally? Yes."

"You think I should let her die."

"You've got to do what's right for yourself and the hell with your family."

"That's just being selfish."

"Not exactly," Raven said. "Haven't you heard the famous quote? 'Every man kills the thing he loves'."

"Quel idee! You're saying I should kill Danielle?"

"What I am saying is don't get obsessed with her. Believe me, if you get obsessed with someone..."

Raven stammered and shook his head. He sank two fingers into the breast pocket of his shirt. When they came up he was holding a piece of hair, a thick black braid, and as if it were a revered object, he slid the palm of his other hand across it, caressing, stroking. He had detached himself from the present moment, it seemed, and his eyes had become a glaze of moisture.

"No," he said, his mouth a grimace. "If you kill the person you love, it may not end your obsession. If you actually do kill that person, it may make your obsession worse. Where do you think I took this hair from? But if I hadn't rid myself of someone, if I hadn't cut loose from her family, I would have been like a slave. That's what you're turning into. A slave to your sister's insanity."

Raven started to twirl the braid and he looked at Charles as if to make sure that he had been understood. Charles thought he had understood, and with the understanding he felt a piercing coldness, a dagger of ice slicing along his spine.

"You've got to break loose no matter what," Raven added.

He was leaning over now, his voice a silky whisper in Charles' ear, and he said point-blank that he had a plan that might interest Charles. And though Charles tuned him out, thinking of his sister and where she might have gone after leaving the boat, he did catch fragments of Raven's proposition. Something about an American girl who was living alone in Fort de France, an American girl who had wealthy parents back in the States. "It would be so easy," Raven concluded. "Using your boat it would be a piece of cake."

Charles laughed in disbelief, but as he pulled away from Raven, as he stepped from the prow to the dock, he saw Raven's face cloud with displeasure.

"You're not kidding me, Paul? This plan of yours is serious?"

"Damn right it's serious."

"A kidnapping, huh?"

"We could make ourselves a lot of money."

"And leave Martinique. We'd have to go."

"That's the whole idea. We'd get off this island and both of us would have the money to go wherever we want."

"I can't desert Danielle like that."

"She's a blonde," said Raven, grinning salaciously. "The girl I'm talking about is a blonde, and not too bad looking either."

"When did you meet her?"

"I haven't yet. But I've been trailing her around town. Seeing what her routine is like."

"A blonde, huh?"

For Charles the word conjured up visions of the actresses he favored, the blonde pornographic queens, and these lascivious faces blended into a composite picture, his image of the girl in question. A blonde captive on his boat? A white girl who they would have under their control? There would be pleasure in that, much pleasure, but forever afterward he would know that he had left Danielle to die.

"It's impossible," he said, beckoning Raven off the boat. "I just can't do it." And while Raven lingered, unwilling to give up his attempt at persuasion, Charles repeated that he had to get home. He had to see whether his sister had returned to their house safely. "My car's by the Abracotier," he said. "Hop in and I'll drive you over to the residence."

*****

He found Danielle lying in her bed, sleeping on her side, worn out from the effort she had expended by walking into town and back. In her exhaustion she had dropped off with the lamp on her reading table alight, and the illumination sifting through the muslin shade lit the half of her face not touching the mattress. Such honey-colored skin she had, such cherubic cheeks, and no barber had ever cut into the kinky thickets of her black hair. Under her upswung skirt, the blue cotton, her thighs were tucked against her stomach and she had her left thumb between her lips. Had she dreamt yet during this sleep? Would she dream of what she had watched on his pornographic videos? The stuff of those films had made a strong impression on her mind, and with Danielle that was a danger because she suffered from periodic nightmares. These had plagued her since her childhood and she still would come running into his room when one of them woke her up. Next to him, she would say, she felt protected from the horrible dreams, and she would get into his bed so that he could hold her.

On the dresser the clock chimed, marking the hour. Through the window screen came the air scented with frangipanni and dew. The neighbor's horrid dog was barking, smitten perhaps with the blood-red moon, and from the shelves around Charles, the black eyes were staring, the black buttons stitched into faces of fur and plastic. Danielle cherished her toy animals, and she had draped her human dolls in colorful handsewn gowns. "This is Catherine and this Jeanne. Here I have the beautiful Charlotte." And she would talk to the figures; she would play with them on the floor. But what would she do if he were to avenge himself by destroying these 'ladies,' these *belles femmes*, if he were to take the pandas, bears and smiling tigers and throw all the dolls on a bonfire? Tomorrow morning, in the backyard, he could conduct the mass immolation of her inanimate companions, and how would she react to that? With another paroxysm of rage, he thought, and she would see no correlation between his action and what she had done to his video tapes. Self-centered, uncomprehending, she would believe he had burned her things out of some unreasonable spite. She would feel bereft of his affection and sob over that for days. No, it would be too cruel, almost sadistic, to punish Danielle for her destructive outburst on *The Lucky Blonde*.

A door hinge rasped, the sole of a slipper knocked against wood, a spear of light came angling into the room. Charles turned from the bed, his back to the muslin-covered lamp, and there in the hall he saw his mother. She had put her hair in curlers before retiring, had wrapped her ponderous body in a green, tentlike robe. Advancing age was giving her face an equine appearance, a snouty and triangular aspect, and when would she shave that peachy fuzz under her nose? "Come talk," she said, with iron authority, and in his hasty exit from the room, Charles forgot to pull the little chain on his sister's lamp.

Once in the passage he shut the door, leaving himself and his mother in darkness. An insect flit round his throat, a moth with sandpaper wings, and he could still hear the moonstruck dog yipping in the neighbor's yard. There was a smell of coconut lotion radiating off his mother, and her voice, though hushed, was uncharacteristically blunt. Speaking in Creole, her language of preference, she asked Charles what had happened on his yacht. An hour or so earlier Danielle had entered the house in tears, and when offered a cup of hot chocolate, her nightly drink, she had declined claiming that she felt queasy. "Salo!," she had said, referring to Charles. "He's not the good boy you think he is."

His mother's bulk looked monstrous in the dark. Pressed against her enormous busom one might choke for lack of oxygen; held in those arms fattened by a diet of starchy foods one might be crushed like an egg.

"Can't this wait?" Charles said, using French. "We don't have to discuss this now."

Because Danielle was unpredictable. Although she had erupted tonight, he could imagine her awaking in a calm frame of mind. He could see her wanting to patch things up with him. She had laid waste to his porno film library, but quite possibly she would realize that nothing would be accomplished by telling their parents about it. Regular attendants at Sunday mass, staunch Catholics already disappointed because he had rejected the church and its dogma, they would regard as perverse and unwholesome the interest he had in video erotica. They would view the matter as a family crisis, as if he had contracted a disease. Charles, the Charles they had raised, a collector of pornographic tapes? How the thought would sadden their conservative souls. He ran the car sales business his father had started, and to them he was the ideal son, the perfect issue, his lapsed religious status notwithstanding.

"Let's go, mom. We'll wake her up talking here."

But had their voices already infringed on the serenity of her sleep? Had the terrifying dreams begun? The dog behind the neighbor's fence had stopped barking and through his sister's door he heard movement, heard Danielle tossing in her bed. Out of her mouth came garbled words, weird babble, something that sounded like "men love sluts, men love women who love to fuck," and then from the abyss of her sleep she produced a succession of sibilant cries. It pained Charles to listen to her, to know that she was once again battling with her psychic demons. Yet he forced himself to stay put, checked himself from rushing inside, and the hand that he clapped on his mother's arm told her not to go in. "It'll pass," he said, steering her toward the end of the hall. "Let her sleep through it if she can." And in the morning, if she was conciliatory, if she had slept off her anger, he would enfold his baby sister in a brotherly hug. He would kiss her till she smiled, and ask her whether she wanted a massage. Nothing enlivened Danielle like his roving touch did, and through his thaumaturgic fingers, he would weave a spell of love, make her forget his collection of videos.

"What's that blood? Did Danielle hit you?"

He and his mother had stepped into the living room, into a swath of dusky light, and there in the wickerwork seat sat his father, the broken man. The bottle and the glass were on the stool beside him, and above the waistband of his boxer shorts his gut hung down like a piece of wilted dough. Once bushy-haired, now bald, he had the eccentric habit of greasing his scalp with olive oil, and he still would wax and trim his mustache. 'Lassitude incarnate,' thought Charles. 'One day he'll be dead and we won't know the difference.' His hands in his lap, his jowls aquiver, the old man was staring at the wall across the floor, looking at the white rectangular surface as if it were a movie screen, a screen throwing back the images of the life he could have had. Rash investments and American swindlers had more than halved his inherited fortune; some of his real estate properties in Florida had gone undeveloped. And Charles, a financially inexperienced Charles, had watched his father run up debts, had worked with him during that time of blunders. It had been maddening. On several deals, deals that would prove calamitious, his father had acted against his advice, and he had felt an unrestrainable glee observing the man's deterioration.

"You have a big bump," said his mother. "You should put something on that."

"It's nothing to worry about."

But his mother insisted on parting his curls, on examining

his head close up.

"Mon Dieu! You don't want to get an infection."

"I won't."

"She must have clubbed you."

"It's a little bruise."

"At least let me clean it with alcohol."

She waddled off, a mother transformed into a nurse, and in his chair the old drunk reached toward the stool and his poison. The liter-sized bottle was a third full, the rum he was drinking an amber color. And he looked dissipated from his inordinate liquor consumption; the skin on his face had the yeasty distention of a waterlogged corpse. Charles watched him lift his glass, turn his wrist, spread his mouth into a waiting oval, and as the rum went down inside him, his neck expanded like a frog's. Months ago, in a joke he shared with his sister, Charles had nicknamed him The Frog, and to his way of thinking the man had outlived his value to their family. A feeble appendage, a pet with a gluttonous appetite, his father existed in a bubble of self-pity, a haze of regrets. He had the obscene belly and the foppish mustache, he had eyes as opaque as any amphibian's, and in the heat of the afternoons he would loaf in the backyard hammock, snoring so loud the neighbors complained. Undone by the world, he had removed himself from it, though every so often he would remember to take an interest in the family business. The impulse to help would seize him then, the energy to work, and in a fairly sober condition he would stop by the car dealership. And this was the business he himself had established, the enterprise he had launched after the fiascos in Florida. As listed in the deeds, the official documents, he still owned the concern, but Charles ran everything now; Charles had become the one responsible for supporting his mother and Danielle.

In a minute she was back, his mother the nurse, and she cooed with sympathy because he had the head wound. She told him to brace himself and he felt the sting from the alcohol, the glancing pressure from the cotton swab. "Ma cherie. Does it burn?" The stupidity of her question riled him, and he hated the mannered tone she had used. "I know it burns, but we don't want you to get an infection."

Lost to everything but his rum, The Frog continued to stare at the white wall. Outside beyond the fence the dog was barking again. Those people next door had the nerve to complain when his father snored in the hammock, yet they refused to muzzle their demented animal. This made Charles' temper rise and he reflected on how he had no privacy in the house, nowhere to go for peace and quiet except his yacht. An island's like a prison, he thought, an island is too confining, and with a pang of nostalgia he remembered Florida. Green and tropical, like Martinique, with palm trees and a blue sky, but there you had room to roam, to get off by yourself and find anonymity. In Martinique, by contrast, somebody knew him, said hello to him, regardless of where he went.

A fresh dose of alcohol caused more burning; he felt his dried blood dissolving into the cotton. And though he said that she had cleaned him up enough, his mother kept dabbing at the bruise, drawing the colorless disinfectant from a cone-shaped flask. She was all concentration, her horsy face quite solemn, and under her nose the bank of fuzz had grown sweaty. Buxom, thickset, immense, his mother seemed a pillar of strength in her green robe; she looked ready to pull him against her breast and squash him in her arms. He considered the idea of familial love and how constricting it could be, and with an insight that depressed him, he knew that his mother would baby him so long as he was the family's provider. The others depended on his health and any trivial wound he incurred was a potential disaster. "Charles, you can't get sick," his mother would say, and he never detected irony in the injunction. Without him working, without him running the car lot, there might be poverty in the house; there might be dinners of stale bread and garlic soup. So from one point of view he was enslaved, as Raven had said, he was in servitude, but his importance to the family demanded that he receive royal treatment. He was bound to the yoke of his familial obligations, and to break that yoke, to leave for good on *The Lucky Blonde*, he would have to hurt not only his sister, but his trusting parents as well.

Buy supplies, get on the boat, hoist anchor. Put the yacht to sea and keep sailing. If he did these simple things he would be gone, but he would have to harden his heart to do them. He could take Raven as an example of someone who had cut his bonds to home, but Raven had done it by killing; Raven had murdered a girl he loved because he had felt entrapped by her family. "Who needs a family?" was Raven's motto, but now Raven had an ulterior motive for saying that: Raven wanted to suck him into his abduction scheme.

An American girl who comes from money, who lives by herself in Fort de France, and she a blonde who could be your first since that blonde on the beach in Florida.

"Done," said his mother, wiping the cotton over his bruise to soak up the excess alcohol. "You'll be fine." And off she went with her mincing steps, the flask and the reddened swabs in her hands.

Slumped in the wicker chair, The Frog was unconscious, and the man from the house next door had finally yelled at the barking dog. It had obeyed him, going silent, and at last Charles felt that he could look forward to bed, that he could end his atrocious night. But as he let out a yawn, as he surrendered to his fatigue, he heard a sound that put him on edge; he heard the voice from down the hall. His sister was talking in her sleep again, and Charles saw himself going to her room, covering her face with a pillow, sitting on the pillow until she suffocated. Death for her would be an escape from unhappiness, from her history of private torments, and she might be one to welcome its approach. "Mercy. This is an act of mercy," he would say, and he would do the job fast.

"Charles?"

She had begun to call him from her room and he heard the latch turn, the door swinging open. Could she know? Had she sensed, through some inner faculty, what he had just been thinking? Mortified, he waited, and then Danielle emerged from the darkness, her arms stretching toward him like an avid lover's.

"You want a slut, Charles? A blonde slut? Is that why you watch those films?"

They were questions asked in a timid voice, but Charles found himself speechless. He felt a heaviness in his chest, an iron block, and both his feet had become stones. In her blue skirt with the lacy straps, his sister was on display, and he could not but admire her svelte shape, her honey-colored skin, the beauty she had.

"You like blondes, don't you? Imagine me as a blonde."

Her hand reached for his pants, her tongue entered his ear, she drove one knee between his legs. Still he could not speak, could not even utter a protesting grunt, and a vise-grip of panic fixed him to his spot. In his embarrassment he looked to the corner, to his father, but he knew he could expect no aid from there. The Frog was too far gone in his drunkenness. "I'm a whore," Danielle said. "I'm a whore like the blondes in your films. Don't you like me again?"

She had put on perfume - attar of roses - and by her breath, which was hitting his face hard, he could judge the level of her excitement. But what had unleashed this fit of desire? What had prompted this transformation from girlish sister to self-degrading lover? "A whore, a whore," she was insisting, and as she went on repeating the word, milking the word for all its seductive power, Charles had the bizarre impression that she was imitating the female characters she had seen on his erotic videos.

"Danielle. My God!"

To the rescue came their mother, befuddlement in her face, and when she stumbled over to them, Danielle collapsed into her arms. He thought she had fainted, blacked out, but from his position behind her he could hear her talking on. She had her cheek to their mother's breast, and with mounting shrillness and hysteria, she described the films he had owned, the collection she had destroyed. The word 'blonde' kept coming up - and the words 'panting sluts' - and above Danielle's black tangle of hair he could see their mother shaking her head at him. Confronted with her gravity, her look of parental censure, he felt abashed and sullied, and yet he wanted to spit in her eyes. The prude! Did his liking for pornographic cinema merit such a reaction? He was a grown man.

Unhinged altogether, Danielle was denouncing the porno stars, the actresses, as if they were her rivals for his affection. And she was doing it at so high a pitch that Charles feared she would awaken some of the neighbors. He crossed the room and walked through the door and outside in the driveway he leaned his elbows against the roof of his car. The air was wet with a soft warm rain, and he knew he would have to go to his boat for solitude.

"He loves blondes, mom. Every film had a blonde. He can't get enough of watching those slutty blondes."

In the neighboring houses lights had come on. People had indeed been awakened. Most certainly they were listening to Danielle and tomorrow they would start their gossip about him.

'They'll say I prefer white girls' he thought, and that led him back to imagining the girl Raven wanted to kidnap. *An American who has rich parents, who has an apartment in Fort de France, and she's a blonde who could be your first since that blonde on*

85

the beach in Miami.

*****

"She comes to the beach almost every Sunday," Raven said.

"By herself? There's no boyfriend?"

"Not that I've seen."

Above them was the sky, blue and clear, below them were the hot grains of sand, and he and Raven had spread their towels within sight of the American girl, Bianca Bishop. She lay on a mat of yellow straw about ten yards to their left, and to make her tan a more complete one, she had removed the top portion of her bikini. The bottom half was black and small, like a stripper's drawers, but with her eyes shut and her hands on her stomach, she looked supremely unselfconscious. On these beaches in Martinique she had heard the whistles and attracted the inane flattery, and none of it was going to inhibit her when she sunbathed.

"It's funny how you see so few Martinicans doing that," Charles said.

"Lying topless?"

"It's the Americans, the French, the Germans...it's like the women coming down to the tropics can't wait for the chance to undress. To get natural."

"So? You shouldn't mind."

Children kept running by in the sand; an infant had started to whine in its mother's lap; two boys in the shallows were giggling and splashing. People covered the long beach, people with their sun creams and detective novels, with their headphones and the miniature cassette players, and Charles listened to the medley of languages being spoken around them: the Parisian French, the Martinican Creole, English, Italian. Sunday drew tourists and locals alike, and here on Trois Ilets, the hotel-filled peninsula, concession stands and refreshment trucks would be doing lots of business. There would be strangers who would glance at him, there would be acquaintances who would stop to exchange hellos, but no one in this crowd out to enjoy the heat and the swimming, the flirtations in the sun, would have any inkling that he had come for a serious purpose, a reconnaisance mission.

"I want you to see her for yourself," Raven had said, and it had been Raven's suggestion that he do his observing at the beach. He had met Raven by the harbor, had sat with him drinking coffee at a bistro, and together they had boarded the packed ferryboat crossing the bay.

"And if she's not there?" Charles had asked. "If she went to do something else?"

"Then it's an hour wasted. But she'll be there. She has her weekly routine."

Yes, she did. She had her untroubled expatriate life - a life funded, Raven had told him, by an allowance from home - but this would end when they took her onto his yacht, when they made her their prisoner. And for him, Charles, she was all that he could have wanted: a roomy-hipped, large-boned girl whose hair was a flaxen shade of blonde.

"You knew I'd be drawn," he said to Raven.

"I thought so."

"If only her face was a little better."

"It's average."

She had arisen from her mat and put her bikini top back on. Smiling affably, pointing down, she asked the white couple on the towel beside her to watch her blue tote bag, and after they had assented with nods, she walked forward into the water. There were no rocks or waves or bits of seaweed, and the mirrorlike smoothness swallowed her up. When she resurfaced, she was out farther; she had propelled herself beyond most of the bathers. Never pausing, Bianca went into a crawl, and she seemed to have the easy technique of a practiced swimmer. She barely disturbed the water as she swam, and with every other overarm stroke, she turned her head to the right so that she could breathe. Formidable, Charles thought, even intimidating; it would not be a simple thing to abduct Bianca Bishop, to overpower her. He remarked on this to Raven, who agreed with him, and when he looked at Bianca again, she was just a blonde speck still moving away from the shore.

"And your friend?" he said, twisting back toward Raven. "He's all ready?"

"Larry's set. I spoke to him on the phone this morning."

"Did you tell him about me?"

"I had to."

"Told him I have a boat?"

"We wouldn't need you if you didn't have the boat."

Raven said this with an impish grin, but he became more earnest when he declared that Larry had his trust, that he and

Larry had gone through fires together.

"The girl I killed? He helped me with that situation."

"Well this is a new one," Charles said. "And I'd like to meet him before we do anything."

"You will. You'll have to when he flies down here, right?"

For the first time Charles could truly foresee his escape from the island. In the life to come he would have no parents to support, no car business to run, none of the encounters with gossiping fools who had known him since he was a child. And Danielle, poor Danielle? Would she do herself harm with him not there? It was a question that unsettled him, and to quiet his conscience he resolved to leave the family savings behind, to leave Danielle and his parents the resources for survival.

"Call up Larry tonight," he said. "Tell him we're waiting."

Out in the water Bianca Bishop had changed her direction and with her effortless strokes, her precise leg kicks, she was returning to the shore.

Chapter Ten

Inside his apartment, his Bronx craphole, Larry was lifting weights to release tension. Things had become snarled for him, priorities confused. The telephone call from Raven, the news that Raven had persuaded his Martinican friend to join them, complicated the dilemma. Tonight, or tomorrow at the latest, he would have to make his choice, and the decision would be guided by the answer to one fundamental question: could he actually do the despicable and turn against Raven? With Raven, who was his best friend, he had a relationship built on mutual trust, and Raven had been the one to bring him into this kidnapping scheme in the first place. 'I know you want to get out of the city, quit your job, get out of that slummy apartment,' Raven had written to him at the time. 'This might be your chance...'

Raven, good old Raven, Larry had thought, and he liked the audacity of Raven's plan. In his letter Raven had described his meeting with the Bishops, had spoken of the wealth they claimed to have, and Larry had done what he could to get close to them. He'd wanted to confirm that they were affluent, that they had the money to pay a big ransom, and to do this he had contrived to insinuate himself into Caroline Bishop's life. But while working with her on her tennis game, while eating with her at restaurants, while lying with her in shabby motel rooms, he had failed to maintain his detachment; he had not kept an aloof frame of mind. He was the spy who had lost his equanimity, the observer who had formed a will-weakening link with the observed. As a result, he felt divided now, and he was holding something back from both Caroline and Raven. Caroline did not know about Raven, and Raven had no idea that he was involved with the mother of their intended victim. Given these particulars, what were his options? He could repress what he felt for Caroline and go to Martinique for the abduction, or he could tell Caroline everything and thus destroy Raven's plan. Either way, he would feel wretched; he would lose somebody important to him.

Despondent, sapped of strength, Larry put down his ten-pound dumbbells. He went into the kitchen for his codeine tablets and swallowed five with a glass of water. The nerves in his jaw, his crooked chin, were not aching this evening, but he was hoping for the solace of a dreamy nod. All through the night he could have rapturous dreams, and later, at some indefinite point later, he would decide what he should do.

For several hours he drifted between consciousness and oblivion. He had a sofa cushion under his head on the living room floor; he had the window open and a fan directed at his body, and as was his usual custom for nods, he was lying in total darkness. Most of the time the darkness helped him give himself over to his imagination, but tonight no enjoyable visions came, just traumatic memories. At certain moments he could hear sounds coming through the wall - laughter, voices, synthesized dance music - and with some segment of his brain, he apprehended what had triggered his recollections. It was the party itself, those uproarious noises in the next apartment, and he wanted to rise, to run, to go somewhere else till the bash ended. Nothing doing; he had too much codeine in him for that, and he stayed on the floor dreaming, thinking, drowning in the flood of images from his past.

These images would never leave him. The house on Long Island, the party thrown by his father's boss, the sky turning black when he was in the yard playing with the other kids - all these things he could remember, and he remembered the kettledrum thunder and the white lightning. His father had drunk beyond his limit that afternoon, and the onset of the rain had worried his mother who knew how the liquor would mar his father's judgment. She asked their host to offer him coffee, which he accepted, and she told him that she would do the driving on the ride home. "Be my guest," his father said. "I don't care." But when the time came for them to go, he refused to hand her the keys and he insisted on taking the wheel himself.

Why hadn't she stopped him? Why had she argued with him, tried to reason with him, and then walked out to the car and sat in the passenger seat? Even now Larry could not understand this, though he believed that his parents had gone through this routine before. His mother and father squabbling over who would drive them home from a party; his father, in the end, getting his way. To his drunken obstinance she would invariably submit, and on that night of wind and rain she had suffered the fatal consequence. She had been killed in the collision with the truck, even though she was wearing her seat belt.

Next door the synthesizer music was pulsing, and the wall between his apartment and that one had begun to vibrate. 'Fucking bastards!' he heard himself yelling, and then he realized he had not spoken; a man in the corridor had, incensed by the noise from the party.

"I got to work in the morning. Some of us in this goddamn building have to sleep."

"Use codeine," Larry said, as if answering, and the drug carried him off again. It took him down into a void. How long he remained there he did not know, but when he awoke he was standing in the dark and could feel the draft from the fan blowing across his legs. What had he gotten up for? 'To see mom,' a voice in his head told him, and he flipped the switch on the living room lamp as he moved toward the bookshelf. On it he had the volumes devoted to handicapping and backgammon strategy, and there, too, stood the photograph album where he preserved the pictures that meant something to him: those of himself before the accident and those of his mother. He went through the section with his mother's photos, regarding her at various ages of her life, and as he reacquainted himself with her appearance - the blondish hair, the hawksharp nose, the brittle smile and the eyes tinged with stoicism - he recalled how it had been his brother, not his father, who had informed him of her death. Bob, seven years older than he was, had elected to skip the Long Island gathering, and Bob had been sitting next to his bed when he'd awakened in the hospital. From under the facial bandages he had listened to his brother; through the gauze and tape he'd cried. But had his brother volunteered to break the news, or had their father asked him to do it? Their father, Bob said, had instructed him to do it, primarily because he was so grief-stricken himself. Hurled from the car when it fishtailed into the truck, their father had nevertheless come out of the crash unscathed.

Larry shut the photograph album and slid it back onto the shelf. The uproar from the neighbor's apartment was continuing, and just to remind the rude people that he was there, he started kicking and banging the wall, screaming at them to lower their music. A butcher's knife came through the plaster, missing his hand by an inch, and above everything else going on, he heard the man in the corridor threatening to phone the police. "Assholes!" Larry shouted. "You assholes!" This was his existence, here in this rattrap, here in this part of the Bronx where shootings and stabbings occurred every night, but he could leave the inferno forever if he did what he'd said he would do and went along with the abduction.

Stymied again by his choice, he walked into the kitchen intending to take another dose of the codeine. He had the pills in a pharmaceutical bottle on the counter, and he thought he would ingest enough of them to knock himself out till the afternoon. Then, as he was passing the table, he looked at his backgammon set (he would study positions and review strategies while eating), and it dawned on him that he could put his faith in chance. He could put himself in the hands of fortune by letting the dice decide things for him. That was the answer - one roll of the bones. Any combination of six or less and he would stay loyal to Raven; seven or more and he would reveal the plan to Caroline, asking her to forgive his participation in it.

Larry sat down. He shook the dice in the square cup, sent them rolling across the triangles on the board. Two! That meant sticking with Raven, snatching the girl, dismissing whatever he felt for Caroline. But he kept thinking of the years he'd spent alone, the shyness that had developed in him after the scarring from the accident. Not since the death of his mother had he been as close to a woman as he was to Caroline; he would always remember the dates that had been fiascos, the gambling winnings he had squandered on prostitutes. Why should he go back to that loneliness? If the abduction succeeded he would have the money to live in the tropics himself, but that old feeling of isolation would be with him again.

In the street, under his window, there was the sound of a police siren arriving. Larry stood up when he heard it and at that moment he concluded that he would tell Caroline, though he would make an enemy of his best friend.

*****

"We both like motel rooms, don't we?"

Caroline laughed and slipped off the bed and Larry watched her glide through the dark to the bathroom. As her hand touched the wall, the fluorescent shaft in there came on, and with the heel of her left foot she closed the door. He heard her pulling the curtain, stepping into the tub, finagling with the clunky taps until the water started to flow. At ease on the sheets they had mussed with their gyrations, he listened to her singing a song, the melody of some song, and he began to ask himself whether she felt any love for her daughter. Two days had gone by since he had told her of the plot, warned her of the danger Bianca was in, but she was comporting herself as if none of it mattered. This baffled Larry and he knew he would have to return to the subject. 'Let Bianca know,' he would say. 'Let her know so she can leave the island in time. I can't guarantee that Raven won't do it with just one partner, the Martinican who has the boat.'

Caroline came back, minty-smelling, damp-skinned, her hair flat and golden against her scalp, and like a lover drunk on love she dove into the bed. She drew up a sheet and pressed in beside him, curled one leg over his. Silence would have been nice, the rest and silence of lying with her and feeling her supple body there, but Larry could not squelch his worries. He began to say what he had thought out and emphasized that Bianca had to be alerted soon.

"Raven expects me in a week," he said. "Use that week to get her home."

Caroline raised her leg off him and propped herself up on one elbow. The sheet had fallen down to her hips and he could see her looking at him with a calculating face.

"Alright," she said. "I want you to listen to me carefully."

"I'm listening."

"Your kidnapping plan? I don't want you to change it."

"Very funny."

"I'm not joking. I want you to go through with it."

"You want your daughter abducted?"

"That's what I'm asking you to do. Yes."

It came as a shock, this request, and Larry let his astonishment show. He felt that he would have to rethink his basic conception of the Bishop family. Until just now he had been sure that the venom in the family was between only Caroline and her husband; he had assumed that Caroline and her daughter got on well. Caroline had never said anything to the contrary, and whenever she had discussed her family with him she had harped on her difficulties with Eric, on her antipathy towards the two East Indian spiritualists her husband was permitting to live with them. Larry could see why she would detest that pair of 'interlopers,' that pair who had 'brainwashed' her husband into following their ascetic precepts, but what could account for the ill-will she evidently bore towards her daughter?

"I don't understand," he said. "Why would you want us to put Bianca through that?"

"For the money," Caroline said.

"What money? The ransom money?"

"The money you'll get and split with me."

"Split with you? Where do you come into this thing?"

Caroline had an answer for him and Larry kissed her on the head acknowledging the cleverness of her idea. To her the question was rhetorical: why should she subject herself to the ghastly process of a divorce trial when she could acquire a hefty wad of her husband's money through the kidnapping? "You and your friends will hold Bianca until you get the ransom money," she said. "Then I'll leave Eric and join you wherever you are. When I said 'split the money with me,' I didn't mean I want a cut of the ransom. I meant I'll join you afterwards and the cut you've taken will belong to us together. To both of us, because we'll be living together. Are you ready for that? Would you want to live with me?"

Larry smiled, reaching for her face, and she edged closer to him on the bed. She had flopped onto her stomach, her chin held up by her interlocked hands, and with the sheet down at her ankles, every inch of her solidness was exposed, a pinkish white against the darkness.

"When we get the news that she's been abducted, I'll have to pretend I'm distraught," she said. "But I'll do it; I'll do an acting job, and I'll see to it that Eric pays."

"Would he hesitate about paying?"

"Not for his darling jewel. Never. He loves Bianca."

"And you don't?" Larry asked.

"I love her. Certainly I do. But there's no law that says a mother can't use her child to help herself."

Caroline had defiance in her voice. She was daring Larry to contradict her. He didn't, fearing that they were on sensitive ground, and then she was forcing a laugh and excusing herself, telling him not to look at her as an evil parent. She wanted no harm to come to Bianca, and she would hold him responsible for how Bianca was treated during her time in captivity.

"I'm willing to let her be used as a pawn, but that's as far as it goes."

"I wouldn't molest her," Larry said.

"Maybe you wouldn't. But can you vouch for your friends?"

"I can for Raven. He's doing this just for the money."

"And the other guy? The Martinican?"

"I'll have to watch him," Larry said. "I don't know him."

"Watch him well then. Because if she comes back injured or says she was raped, I'll do everything I can to see you hunted down."

That settled that. They had forged the terms of their understanding. Any mother who would let her child experience the terror of a kidnapping had the ruthlessness of Medea in her, and Larry believed her when she said that she would become his avenging pursuer if Bianca got hurt by him or his partners. For as long as they had Bianca, he would have to be her guardian, though he would have to fulfill that role without seeming unduly concerned for her welfare. This would put him at risk until they released the girl, but under no circumstances could he allow his partners to ascertain what he had going with Caroline. Even Raven would distrust him if he learned about Caroline, and distrust among people in a venture so perilous could lead to violent dissention, violent acts.

"Should we go?" Caroline said. "This motel is always damp."

Tonight more so than usual (because of the dankness his jaw was throbbing), and there was a faintly septic stench arising from the bathroom pipes. No one looking for a place with class would have met at this motel, but over the course of their rendezvous here, he and Caroline had grown fond of its tawdriness. The Comfort Nest, as it was named, stood halfway between where each of them lived, and in every room they could count on finding Chinese lanterns and tasselled curtains, velveteen pillows and tacky carpets.

"And if all goes well?" Larry said. "If everything goes according to plan? Where would you want to meet?"

"Jamaica, maybe. Bermuda."

"How about Nice? The French Riviera."

"Sounds good," Caroline said. "Very glamorous."

"I'd like to see the casinos there."

"The casinos? That's out. I'll leave in a second if you start gambling with that money."

Again a threat, an exacting demand, but through this one she transmitted an unequivocal warmth, a kind of maternal solicitude. Larry liked that, something in him responded to that, and he swore that he would try to avoid the blackjack tables.

"I quit smoking for you," said Caroline. "You can make yourself give up gambling."

Sure he could, of course he could; to forego the stimulation of gambling would be a trifling sacrifice for the privilege of living with Caroline. Larry held his right hand up as if he were holding a champagne glass, and with a grave deliberateness, he went through the conventional motions of a person drinking a toast.

"To lovers," he said. "To lovers who live on the French Riviera."

He heard the tread of feet passing in the hall and down below their balcony. Down in the motel parking lot, the voice of a man screeched with outrage. Larry thought that somebody's car had run into somebody else's, and to see what promised to be a quarrel, he lifted himself off the bed and went buck-naked to the sliding window. He had opened it earlier to let in some air, to provide ventilation for himself and Caroline, and as he stepped through the part between the two halves of the purple-red curtain he could smell hot sugar cooking in the ovens of the donut shop across the road. The night distracted him with its moon, a lurid golden saucer of a moon, but then he saw the three-forked prong attached to the grillework on their balcony. It must have been a mountain climber's hook and corded hands were pulling themselves up the rope suspended from it. Into his view came black hair cut in the shape of a mushroom cap, a swarthy face with a VanDyke beard, the barrel chest of a miniature man wearing nothing but white pants. As Larry knew, this was the midget, this the assistant to Eric Bishop's Indian swami, and he jumped forward to defend himself from the attack. He snatched at the hook in an effort to disengage it, but the midget was already off the rope, his stunted body spinning through the air. The heels went up and over the head, the arms extended like the wings of a bird, the face that was upside down before Larry grinned at him with blatant arrogance. Mesmerized by those acrobatics, Larry stood by flat-footed, and the perfection of the flying somersault brought the midget to rest on the balcony, his landing as soft and balanced as a gymnast's.

"Thief!" cried the man down below. "We've got a thief in room 27."

That was the man from the front desk (Larry could now recognize the voice), but his call of alarm seemed absurdly late. The midget was invading the sexual sanctum that he and

Caroline had found, and like a commando with orders to maim, not kill, the little typhoon of a man sprang toward him shooting a karate chop to his knee. Larry went down, fell onto his side, and he knew only the pain that he felt. He saw himself walking with a limp, encumbered by a dead leg, and in his eyes he felt the tears caused by the pain. "Little freak. Little monkey." But the midget had not finished with him yet, and before he could raise his arms to protect himself, there was a hammer blow of a kick, the sole of the hard tiny foot striking deep into his midriff. Numbness began to spread through him, a numbness that made it impossible to move, and breathing itself became a memory since his lungs refused to draw air. He had been kicked in the diaphragm, the solar plexus, and he could not summon the voice to warn Caroline.

What would the midget do? Had he been sent by a jealous Eric to frighten Caroline, or had he come, physical marvel that he was, to injure the two of them? Somehow he had driven himself from the Bishop house in Westchester, somehow he had followed Caroline without her seeing him in her rearview mirror, and the rope with the three-forked prong was not all that he had brought with him for his task. Jingling in his pants, as Larry could hear, was something metallic, and through the thickening mist in his eyes, Larry saw him reach for his hip and unbutton a pouch that bulged in the white lining. Out came a set of handcuffs, then another, and above his immobilized head the midget dangled what he held, twirled the manacles one to a hand. As before, he was grinning (though his VanDyke beard and the glow from the moon gave his grin a devilish character), and biding his time, chuckling with the humor of a sadist, he laid his hands, with the manacles, over Larry's face.

Larry ordered himself to rise. He spoke to himself within himself like a fallen boxer trying to beat the count of ten. But nothing he said to his muscles availed him; nothing he signalled with his brain put new air into his lungs. For these torturous seconds he was a mind separated from his body, and he felt himself unable to resist when the midget's hand grabbed his shoulder, delved underneath his back, started to turn him onto his stomach as if he were an animal soon to be slaughtered. Then he had his chest to the concrete, his chest and his stomach and his sore chin, and he could feel the cold and the hardness jammed against his groin. Behind his back, a foot to his spine, the midget pulled and straightened his arms, and as it went with his wrists, so it went with his ankles, each click of the iron rings locking him into his humiliation.

The curtain fluttered, the part down its middle widened. In the opening appeared a leg, pink and firm, bare from foot to thigh, and by twisting his neck and screwing up his eyes, Larry could see the face of Caroline, her wet blonde hair and shapely cheeks framed by the purple and red of the cloth.

"Larry! What's going on?"

Her panic-throttled voice had no strength in it, no resonance, and with the urgency in his expression, Larry tried to tell her that she should run, that she should leave him as he was and not engage in battle with the midget. It seemed, from her nod, that she understood him and back she went through the split in the curtain while the vigorous midget sprang past his head in pursuit. A silver tassel on the drapes shook, dust flew up from the edge of the room, and Larry banged his chin on the concrete as he struggled against his fetters. Now he had a searing pain in his jaw as well as in his knee, and though he could breathe again, and thus move again, he found himself gagging on a line of blood flowing from the end of his tongue. In that spot, while squirming in the handcuffs, he had bitten himself; he had wounded himself in his frustration over his helpless position. He had the smell of the balcony dust in his nose and that sugary smell from the baking donuts, and inside the room, behind the curtain, Caroline had just begun to scream. But this, her scream, did not go on for long; as loud as it started, it abruptly stopped. The midget had put a hand to her mouth or a pillow to her face, or perhaps had delivered a karate blow to her throat, and the silence that resulted was worse than the shrillest of her screams could have sounded. The silence told Larry that she was hurt, or even dead, for who having seen him in action could deny that the midget had lethal weapons for hands? The midget was one of those people who could target the critical points on the body, the death points, and Larry expected the midget's hands to fall on him again, though they would fall this time with deadly intent.

His head on its side, his eyes squeezed shut, Larry waited for the stroke that would hit him like an axe. He waited for the end, for the breaking of his neck, but then he felt a pushing at his lips and the softness of a towel stuffing his mouth. Is that how the midget intended to kill him? Through the slow torture of asphyxiation? Over his face, he now saw, were the two wiry forearms, and he began to bite at the prying fingers while turning and tossing his head. Quick to react, the midget took his hands away and Larry realized that his goal had been merely to apply a muzzle. Whatever his ultimate plan, the midget was not going to kill him yet, and having secured the towel where he wanted, he went running back through the curtain.

Larry rested his head on the concrete. He tried to reduce the tension in his body so that he could lie relaxed in his bonds. But who could accept chains on one's ankles and chains on one's wrists, and who could tolerate lying naked like a slave in some medieval tyrant's dungeon? The night had become an unrelenting wind carrying dampness that made him tremble, and with the towel stuffed in his mouth he had to take each breath through his nose even as he swallowed the blood from his tongue. He thought of his codeine tablets and how he would need them if he survived this abasement, and then he began to think of Raven. Raven down there in Martinique. Raven who was awaiting his arrival so they could kidnap Caroline's daughter. But had Caroline deceived him? Had she told her husband about the proposed abduction? Maybe this assault by the midget had nothing to do with Eric's anger over his wife's infidelity; maybe it was connected to his own designs on Bianca Bishop. For two days now Caroline had known of the kidnapping plot and she might have been talking disingenuously when she had expressed approval for it. What if she and Eric had called a truce because of his threat to Bianca, and what if they had set up the midget's attack together, with Caroline affecting panic at his appearance? The karate expert would do what he had been asked to do tonight, and after that he would go south to pay both Raven and the Martinican partner a visit. Everything was ruined, everything in the elaborate project had unraveled, and Larry swore at himself for having created the mess. Because of his emotional failing, the need he had developed for Caroline, he had put his oldest friend's life in jeopardy, and nothing but death would be a fit punishment for him. Nothing other than death would suffice, and when he saw the doleful face of Eric above him, the shadowed eyes and puritannical mouth of Eric, he began to wonder who, if anyone, would attend his funeral.

But where had Eric Bishop come from? How had he gotten into the room? It must have been through the regular entrance, the door to the hall, and Larry knew what that meant: Eric had relied on his wealth to buy the indifference of the motel's desk man. The man who had seen the midget climbing up the rope to the balcony, the man who had shouted 'thief' - this man had taken Eric's money promising not to phone the police. Neither would he interfere himself, and if things were kept quiet and clean no one would know anything had happened. That, Larry thought, is what the man had said, and so here was Eric bending over him, scrutinizing him as if he were a crippled ant.

"Hard to believe you're Larry. You don't look like much."

Eric picked him up by his shoulders, the midget by his ankles. And Larry listened to his handcuffs rattling, watched the loose end of the towel dragging over the concrete. Inside the room, along one wall, the Chinese lanterns were on, red, blue, orange, yellow, and as they were moving him across the floor, Larry saw that something green, a large piece of material, was spread in the center of the white carpet. "We'll put you right here," said Eric, and down Larry went onto the material, his weight on his chest and stomach again. Whatever he lay on had a cool feel and from its slickness, its glossiness, he thought it must be a waterproof tarp. It crackled beneath him, released its dust, and near his head he could see two metal buckets. Each had a curved handle attached, and one had a shaft of wood sticking up over its top. But was this shaft a handle in itself, the handle for a tool inside that bucket? Was it the grip for some cutting instrument that would spill his blood onto the convenient tarp? Limb by limb they would take him apart and carry him off, and with a frantic rolling of his body he tried to locate Caroline, tried to find where in the room she had gone. He had nothing but the use of his eyes left to him, but with his eyes he could beseech Caroline's mercy. He could ask that she have the midget kill him with one painless karate chop to his neck.

And she was there, she was close, she was on his right and sitting on the bed. But Larry saw that he had misjudged her. Naked like him, gagged like him, Caroline had her knees to her chest and her chin on her knees, and atop her golden-haired head she had her hands clasped under the blade of the scimitar held by the man standing behind her on the mattress. The man was Eric's personal yogi, the Indian Ashok, his portliness cloaked in Western-style garb -- flannel pants, a beige pullover, even a blue golfing hat -- and underneath the beard that grew in all directions, he looked eerily unperturbed. So did the midget, squatting on his haunches by the foot of the bed, rubbing one hand over his chiseled pectorals, and from these looks of heartless calm, Larry concluded that Ashok and the midget had been in extreme situations like this before. Spiritually-minded or not, they were a diabolic pair, and violence was nothing new for either of them.

"She has to watch this," Eric said. "I want her to remember this."

The all-black clothes, the reed-thin build, the eyes aflame with hatred in the face as bony as a skull - who could have looked more like a bringer of death than Eric? Eric was an executioner without a mask, and from beside the tarp he reached for one of the buckets, grabbed for the shaft of wood sticking upright. Then Larry saw Caroline falling, keeling over on the bed, and her face became hidden in the whiteness of a pillow. Had she fainted? For one or two seconds the guru stood staring at her, stood with his legs well apart and the scimitar held straight out in his hands, and then Eric turned to see what had happened - and in his hand he had the axe that he had lifted from the bucket.

"If she fainted, wake her up. I want her up."

Limb by limb Eric would do it, and on the green tarp the pools of ruby-red blood would collect, and what would Raven be thinking in Martinique? Larry knew that Raven would fume and fret because of the cut-off in communication, but if Eric spared Caroline, as he seemed inclined to do, then maybe she would get a message to Raven. And the abduction? It could be done. Raven could do it with the Martinican guy. But where did Caroline fit into that, and would Raven now want to kill Bianca Bishop even if Eric paid the ransom for the return of his daughter?

"I'm sick of it," Eric said. "Sick of the parade of lovers she's had."

He clucked his tongue and ground his teeth into his lower lip, and behind him on the bed, the corpulent guru had a hold on Caroline's hair. Ashok had taken her by the hair to yank her head up from the pillow, and seeing that she was conscious, that she was trying to avoid looking at Larry, he put the scimitar to her throat and told her to keep her eyes open. As Eric dropped to his knees, raising the hatchet, Larry heard her smothered scream coming through the gag, and for one last time he surveyed her face, pale as ivory and drenched with tears.

..

Chapter Eleven

Another night in Fort de France, another night spent alone with a book, and under the lamp next to her bed Bianca stared at the novel's cover, a drawing of a windswept man and woman embracing on a cliff above the sea. The novel had ended in a predictable way, with the valorous hero rescuing the woman who loved him, saving her from a woeful existence with the debauched viscount, but Bianca did not read these romances hoping to find inventiveness. She read them for the gothic trappings and the momentous passions, and on reaching the final page of a story she would feel a trifle sad. The final page of a good book marked the end of a strong vicarious experience, and without any fictional life to live through, she had to concentrate on her own, and the solitude that went with it. Still, why worry? After the months of lessons and study, she could read French, and tomorrow she would go to one of the bookstores in town. She would buy her next volume of enthralling trash, either a French original or a translation from English, and until she came to the denouement of that one, her mind would be filled with the shivery doings of the innocent girl in danger.

Bianca put the book aside. She turned off the lamp. On the table by the bed she had a bottle of French mineral water, and from its mouth she drank lustily, cooling her throat like a traveler in the desert. The bedsheet, washed that morning in the laundry, felt wonderfully crisp against her skin, but she knew that after a night or two the sweat that she shed during her sleep would soak right into the linen. That was how it was in the tropics, and tonight, she remembered, she had left the portable fan in the living room. Much as she wanted to move the fan, to have it near her while she slept, she did not have the energy to rise from the bed, and so already she was anticipating the shower she would need when she awoke. Nothing but a shower cold as razors got her engines started in the morning, and sometimes she bathed three times a day, loathing as she did the smells she exuded from her pores.

But what was going on? Where was the cat? Around this

time Gussy would appear and leap onto the bed. Gussy would come to rest in her arms. A neighbor overburdened with kittens had given her one some months earlier, had brought her a newborn male, and week by week she had watched him grow on the milk and the gutted fish she served him. She viewed him now as her bosom companion, her one true island friend, and while falling asleep she would hold him beside her petting the downy fur. Because of his color, an inklike black, he would frighten little children when he roamed past them in the street, but in actuality he was a doll, with none of the insolence, the growling haughtiness, common to domestic cats.

"Gussy. Gussy."

She cooed to her pet, tried to entice him onto the bed with whistles. And up onto the sheet he came, snuggling into her arms. Yet she sensed fear in Gussy, fear in the prickliness of his fur and in the pronounced arch of his spine, and standing him up on his hind legs she looked directly into his face. His ears were flattened, his whiskers stiff, his features constricted into a mask of aggression. "What's wrong, Gussy? What frightened you? It couldn't just be a big waterbug, could it?" But Gussy was off, tearing loose, and after he had leaped out into the dark, Bianca heard him running across the floor to the doorway. He hissed like a snake, the sound full of warning, and in the living room he started to scratch at what she thought was the windowpane. Was something outside in the bushes? Something so quiet she could not hear it? Bianca listened as his paws scraped the glass, as his movements rattled the casement, and she herself began to feel frightened remembering that she had left the window open a crack that evening. This was her custom. Burglers were infrequent in Fort de France, and even though her apartment was at street level she would go to bed with her windows open. She would leave every window open a notch to generate a cross-current of air, and that current, regardless of whether she used the fan, would enable her to sleep in adequate comfort.

Yet there could be no sleep with the cat making noise. Bianca rose, despite her torpor, and in her undershirt and her panties over she went to the living room window. Gussy had jumped up onto the sill and Bianca saw that he was jabbing at the bottom part of the window frame, trying to force the sash up so that he could squeeze through the opening. Bent forward, her hands on the glass, Bianca looked out into the night, but all she could see under the stars were the bushes and vines behind the building, the untouched bracken on the lip of the slope descending toward the canal. Had Gussy seen a cat he knew as an enemy? Had a person been creeping through those bushes? Gussy wanted to run outside and chase something, and as he resumed his baleful hissing, Bianca recalled how he had acted during the week long stay by her parents. That had been a time when Gussy was petulant, when Gussy moped underneath the couch and bristled at all her caresses, and during the visit he and her mother had skirmished repeatedly. Her mother disliked pets and was allergic to cats, and she'd accused Bianca of acquiring Gussy solely to prevent her from staying at the apartment. But to prove that nothing could put her off, her mother had sneezed and sniffled for a week; she'd slapped or kicked at Gussy whenever he came too close to her.

One day, in retaliation, Gussy had bitten her on the wrist, and as the blood dripped from her vein, her mother had thrown a pan of boiling water at him, scalding him along his back. "That bitch," Bianca said, thinking of the agonized squeals he had made. "That cruel bitch." In Gussy's mind, she imagined, the episode would never be forgotten, but surely Gussy had not seen her mother in the bushes. Why would her mother be in Martinique? Her mother was at home with her father and no doubt she was having her fun, indulging in her appetite for male flesh.

"Nothing there," Bianca said, tousling the fur under Gussy's chin. "Not a person, not an animal. I don't know what you saw."

She took Gussy into the cradle of her hands and as he mewed and clawed the air, she carried him toward the kitchen to feed him. Food might distract him and make him sleepy, and she herself could do with a sandwich before she returned to bed.

For Gussy, tuna diced into cubes, laid on a dish, and for herself Camembert cheese, wedged into the end of the baguette she had bought to go with her dinner. Gussy was lying up on the table, dining in the place across from her seat, and next to her napkin and her glass she had a bottle of cold rose'. She ate and drank by candlelight, a blue-orange brightness, and the shadow of Gussy cast by the flame covered the shelves opposite her. Taken with the meal, Gussy had stopped looking at the window, but now Bianca was agitated because indeed she could think of a person who might have been lurking in the bushes. Nearby in town lived that American, the young guy with the tan skin, and until no more than a week ago he had been following her around.

When had he started? For how long had he been doing it before she observed him? Too often for coincidence she had seen him in the markets, on the buses, at the beaches, and not infrequently she had spotted him sitting in the same cafe as herself, drinking a coffee and eating a croissant, perusing *The Herald Tribune*. He had curly black hair and the eyes of a restless man, and sometimes she felt like a bug under glass knowing those eyes were pinned on her as she walked the congested streets. In a metropolis, a New York or Paris, he might have been able to follow her like a detective, invisible, unobtrusive, a faceless body among the hordes; but here on this island, in a city this small, who but the most skilled of pros could watch someone for a period of weeks and expect to remain unnoticed? The American, whatever his purpose, did not seem like a professional surveillance man, and Bianca thought he must be a man struggling with an infatuation.

He has a crush. He wants me. He sees that I'm an American, like him. He sees that I'm alone, but he's too shy to approach.

Bianca had seen him once at the supermarket, a bag full of groceries in his arms, and by keeping herself well behind him she had become the person watching, following him to where he lived. That, she discovered, was the residence where her parents had slept one night, and from this knowledge she drew the conclusion that he had met them. He must have met them and they would have spoken of her glowingly, recounting none of the events that had driven her into this exile. Both her parents always told strangers fairy tale stories, stories about the exemplary daughter they wanted others to think they had, and because the American was a compatriot they would have given him her address in Fort de France.

I have a discreet admirer. Isn't that nice? It's like in a novel. But couldn't he also be deranged? Living in that residence as he does he must have a seedy room, and he might be someone very obsessive, someone who spends hours dreaming, a guy who wishes that he could get me alone somewhere. Chloroform and a car and off we'd go, him and me, and he would take me into the forest where no one would hear my cries for help.

Gussy mewed. He swung his tail up and over the candle

flame. Done with the tuna, his plate licked clean, he had arisen on all fours, and on the table pitted with the scratches that he had made over months with his claws he was walking back and forth as if gripped again by the spirit of aggression. Bianca looked toward the living room window fearing that she would see a face, the staid lonely face of the American, but out past the glass she saw nothing, just a square of the night's darkness.

"Gussy, you jerk. You're making me nervous."

Milk is what he needed, a bowl of milk, and Bianca got up to open the refrigerator. She poured from the carton and set the blue bowl in his path and as she had hoped, he came to a stop, dipping his head and starting to drink.

"Isn't that good? You paranoid cat."

But Gussy, she knew, must have seen someone; it seemed highly unlikely that her cat suffered from anything like delusions. To her window on this night there had come a silent prowler and Bianca thought it could not be anyone but the American, hungry to get inside and into her bed. Would she have to sleep with a knife under her pillow?

Gussy was lapping the milk, purring with contentment, and she herself had the cold wine along with the cheese and bread. Everything mixed well in her mouth, the rose' dry, the Camembert tart, the evening's baguette still soft, but she could not enjoy what she had because of the questions in her mind. Until she learned the American's intentions she would feel the ferment of anxiety, and now, out of nowhere, she had formed a new question: what if the American actually was a professional, a detective who had been hired by her mother? What if her mother had sent the man so that from New York she could keep strict tabs on her daughter's Caribbean sex life? Her mother would want to know how she was doing with the boys down here, and whether she had made any conquests yet. From the American, her mother would want descriptions of the boys she had as friends, and when her mother found out that she had no boyfriends, her mother would laugh and feel superior, unmoved by her daughter's inadequacies. But why did her mother have this competitiveness? Why did she have to have a mother determined to act half her age when it came to seducing men, who for neurotic reasons of her own could not bear to see her daughter hit it off with the guys. Up at home, Bianca remembered, her mother had often called her drab, unexceptional, unprepossessing in every sense, and what she thought of as a stalwart body, a shipshape figure, her mother had derided as overly muscular, not feminine enough for a woman's build.

I'm no Snow White, but she has the attitude of Snow White's stepmother.

And who, objectively speaking, was prettier? Bianca could acknowledge to herself that her mother had the clearer skin and the finer cheekbones, that her own brown eyes, inherited from her father, were not as lovely as her mother's green eyes, but did any of this excuse her mother's vanity? Only a mother fixated on competition would pursue her daughter's boyfriend and Bianca still had trouble believing what had happened with Tom. She had loved and trusted Tom and yet her mother, the sexual carnivore, had gone after him. And her mother had seduced him. For several months Bianca had shared Tom with her mother, but she had not even known this until that final night. Something that Tom said to her had clued her into the affair, and with the worst of fears in her heart, she had resorted to a deception, letting her mother and Tom think that she was going to visit a girlfriend. Instead, that night, she had driven to a restaurant and waited, and when she'd thought the time was ripe, she had walked over to Tom's apartment and used her key to slip inside.

How she remembered it; standing there at the entrance to the bedroom, looking in at Tom's pink buttocks and her mother's upraised feet. There were blue high heels on those feet and covering the legs wrapped around Tom's back, red stockings designed like mesh. It had seemed so sordid, Bianca recalled, so brazenly down and dirty, and in the lamp upon the dresser there had been a red bulb.

"You two are a perfect match. Two pigs."

She could still hear herself saying the trite words and from Tom's mouth had come a groan, a contemptible plaint of embarrassment. Yet he neither turned nor lifted his body, and her mother, staring over his shoulder, smiled like a person who had won an athletic contest. In that smile Bianca saw her disparagement, her salacious exultation, and as if to show with a simple gesture how she had control of Tom, she kept his face pressed against her neck even as she stroked with her other hand the black mop that was his hair.

And then came the laughing, her mother's chortles, and her mother was saying that Tom preferred her because Bianca had all the talent of a corpse in bed. It continued like that, with Tom laughing too, shaking in the clutch of her mother's legs, and Bianca felt excruciating spasms kniving through the pit of her stomach. Her head grew light and her vision dimmed, but through her whirling tunnel of fog she noticed the scissors on Tom's dresser; she ran toward the shears with the keen-edged blades. "No!" said her mother. "Don't be stupid." But in this also she met with failure because the person she wanted to stab was her mother and all she remembered at the end of the madness was the blood pouring out from Tom's side, the grissly redness staining the sheets while Tom wept and begged her to stop. Criminal charges? They could have resulted, but perhaps to avoid a public circus, Tom and his parents took the settlement offered to them by her father, the money that would pay for Tom's medical bills and would help finance his law school tuition.

That was the family tragedy, if such could be said of it, and Bianca had never had contact with Tom again. Her mother had gone to the unprecedented length of asking her forgiveness, but rather than attempt to forge a rapprochement, Bianca had suggested to her father that she escape into this exile, go abroad for a change of scene. "I hope it'll help," he had said, kissing her sadly, and he had told her the allowance would come every month for as long a time as she needed it. Bianca felt lucky to have him as her father, to have him as a counterweight to her mother, but what she could not begin to fathom was why he had not divorced her mother years and years earlier. He himself had peculiarities - what else but this could she think? - and he seemed to be getting more eccentric as he passed into middle age.

In recent months, for instance, he had been devoting himself to Indian spiritualism, studying under an Indian swami and that swami's partner. Bianca knew this from his letters and from what he'd said when he and her witch of a mother visited, and in his last letter he had said that the marriage between him and her mother was finally at an end. He'd hinted at a new sexual mess, another outrageous transgression by her mother, and he had written that he was about to leave the United States. In the Indian Ocean, off the coast of Sri Lanka, there was an island he would buy, and on this island not even mapped he would live with his two Indian mentors. Alone with them in this environment he would be like a man in a cloister, and that would free him from distractions so that he could concentrate fully on his yoga.

"But what's his goal?" Bianca said, raising the bottle of rose' wine and tilting the neck over her glass. "What is he trying to accomplish?"

She had a picture of him, ramrod-straight, hard as a rail, sitting on a cushion in the lotus position, and she could not piece this together with her memories of him from other times, the carefree days when she was a child and they were living in southern California. They had been a close-knit family then, cohesive and functional despite the casualness of their life, and her father had been a man who surfed, who smoked marijuana on the beach. He had been a person reacting against the mechanical life that had earned him his fortune, but to go from that brand of iconoclasm to this one, to replace that engaging style of waywardness with this monkish retreat from the world, was, in her eyes, a preposterous step, too radical a metamorphosis. Their family had splintered, fragmented, come apart at the seams, and Bianca felt an orphan's desolation whenever she began to think of that. In their family the one bond left was between herself and her father, but he on his island might push her from his thoughts as he channeled all of his energies into the rigors of his spiritual program. Her allowance would arrive once a month, yet he himself would be unreachable on that island that had no telephone. He would be someone she could talk to only when she dreamt of him, and she wished that she could know beforehand what would happen to his personality under the sway of his two guides. Were they as well-meaning as he believed, those two, or were they using him and his wealth to secure a private paradise for themselves? On that island, alone with them, he might become their entranced prisoner, and Bianca decided she would have to call him before he finalized his plans. She would have to tell him that she was skeptical of the men in whom he had put his trust. But was it too late to sound an alarm? As their disciple, could her father permit himself to doubt their motives?

Questions, Bianca had a slew of questions in her head, and despite the wine that she had drunk, she felt energetic. She felt revivified. The candle on the table had burnt down into a glob of orange wax, Gussy had finished his bowl of milk and coiled himself up to rest, and somewhere in Fort de France, somewhere in the empty narrow streets, a dog was howling as if in the throes of death. Perhaps while searching the gutters for food, while sniffing through the garbage and the slop, it had fought with a rival dog, and lost.

Bianca got up and walked to the living room window again. She peered again at the bushes and vines entangled behind her building. The stars over Fort de France looked like crystals, crystals set on a black canvas, and up in one corner of the window frame, she saw a fly with jade blue wings caught in a perfect circular cobweb. How had she missed seeing that before? The fly had landed in the center of the white net and at the edge of the trap, waiting while the fly twitched and thrashed, sat a gigantic black spider. "No chance," Bianca said, as if the fly would understand. "You've had it." And the stark little drama of life and death, capture and bondage, reminded her that she too might be facing danger, that she might become the prey of the American who had been following her around. With regard to him, she remained at square one, and she wondered how she could somehow learn whether he was working for her mother, sending her mother reports on her life, or whether he was a man obsessed, a man infatuated, a man who would want to have her as helpless as this spider had this fly.

Bianca sulked. Bianca mused. She raised her hand up to the cobweb and tore it apart with a prick of her thumb. The fly and the spider fell past her eyes, the stringy white threads floated in the air, and out of the blue, out of the muddle of her reflections, Bianca thought of an offensive tactic that seemed the best possible course of action. Straightaway, after getting dressed, she could go down the hill and across the canal and confront the American in his residence. She could tell him that the game was up and demand to know why he had been on her tail. At this hour he would be asleep, and so off his guard, and a verbal assault of scathing intensity might leave him cowed. It might dissuade him from continuing his stalking habits. To be sure, if he was obsessed with her, he might respond with violence, enraged that she knew of his passionate feelings, but come what may, Bianca intended to act, to throw off the shackles of her passivity.

Streets with no people and no moving cars, shedlike houses dark as coffins and just as quiet, across the shopfronts metal shutters catching the light from the lamps on the sidewalks - for Bianca the city so vibrant by day became a dismal place in the night, a zone with no more depth and

110

substance than a tenebrous scene from a nightmare. She began to run, to bounce along, her jogging shoes cushioning the force of her steps, and only after she had traversed the yellow arching bridge over the canal and then gone past the peak-roofed enclosure that was, in the day, the central fish market, only after she had turned left and onto the Place Jose Marti, with the long white wall of the cemetery on her right, tombs and crosses grouped behind it, vaults embellished with scrolls and carvings and plaques and flowers, only when she had slowed down and resumed walking, sweat already in her khaki blouse and in the waistband of her jeans, did she notice the presence of Gussy, hastening along at her side. The run, to all appearances, had not tired him, but once again he had in his body the stiffness of a cat geared for aggression.

Bianca stopped, saying his name. She bent toward Gussy to sweep him into her arms. But Gussy sped on as if he knew her destination, or as if at this distance from the residence he had picked up the trail of the scent belonging to the person he despised, the person he had seen outside her window earlier during the night. That had been the American then, no question of it, and Gussy, her loyal Gussy, was more bloodhound than cat. As she proceeded herself, running through the residence parking lot, climbing a flight of wooden stairs, hurrying along a bulb-lit stretch of the interior terrace, Bianca steadied herself for the stress to come. But in the back of her mind she started to think that she should have brought a knife or razor. The American was an unknown quantity who might blow a fuse when she confronted him, and she had nothing in her hands or pockets that she could utilize as a protective weapon.

Postpone her approach? Return to the apartment? Do everything tomorrow night? Bianca said no, she wanted to see the American now, and at the gate of green bars, she put her finger on the buzzer. Gussy himself could have skipped ahead by maneuvering under the lowest bar, yet he stood still and waited for admittance as if their entrance had to be accomplished in concert, a coordinated double-action. Though sorry for her intrusiveness, Bianca kept ringing the bell, and after a couple of long minutes, somebody did walk through the doorway and onto the terrace. It was a student, perhaps, his eyes glassy from interrupted sleep, and as he came toward the gate, he tightened and tied the white string holding up his pajama pants.

111

"Le Americain," said Bianca, and she clarified this by adding that she meant the American guy who had been in the residence for months.

The student said Room 13, at the very end of the left-hand corridor, and even while letting her in with his key, he looked at her with a cynical face. She might have come for hired sex or to complete a drug transaction.

Room 13 had a brown door with painted white numbers, and taped in the center was a white card with the name 'Paul Raven' written across it in blue ink. She heard a door in the passage closing softly - the student re-entering his room - and she could see by the ceiling light the mirror in the wall to her side. As she knocked with her fist, she felt that she had the American cornered, but if that was so, why had Gussy stopped at the neighboring door, the door to Room 12? What was he smelling? Gussy had begun to ram that door, to prod and butt it as if he could smell the American behind it, and yet when Raven's door opened he himself was standing there, stubble-chinned but clear-eyed, clothed in a worn shirt and trousers. "You!" he said in a ghostly voice, but before she could start her intended tirade, the other door opened and Gussy ran in hissing with hatred. Bianca stepped back to take a look into Room 12, and even in the weak light from above, she could distinguish the blonde coif and the old satin robe of her mother. The witch was here, plotting something with her spy, and in retrospect it seemed indisputable that what Gussy had been following was not the scent of the American, but the scent of the woman who had once burned him with boiling water.

"Get him off me," her mother said. "Get him out."

But neither Bianca nor the American did anything to give her help and nothing could prevent the intelligent cat from trying to have his revenge. Despite her hands, her attempted slaps, he used his claws to climb her robe, and once he had pulled himself to her shoulder, he made a direct jump for her eyes. Bianca saw a frenzy of movement and a spurt of dark liquid on her mother's brow, and she was so glad to see her mother get cut that she neglected to watch the American, who had knelt down in his room. When he came forward again, lunging forward, Bianca glimpsed the metal in his hand, and some instinct for self-preservation told her to duck. Too late, too slow; the metal thing hit her flush on the temple. The rug in the passage slanted up toward her face, olive-green, dust-covered, and as the pain went through her head, a curtain of blackness began to descend. She knew she had lost control of her legs. Inside Room 12 it seemed that her mother had managed to grab Gussy's tail, and even from the floor, when she had fallen, Bianca could see her mother spinning, building up speed to smash Gussy's skull against the wall.

But then the curtain fell over everything, its blackness absolute, and she might have been dreaming when she thought 'I am the fly who walked straight into the spider's web.'

Chapter Twelve

Hot in the chest, dry in the throat, Raven made it to the top of the hill. He stepped off the road. A car went past, chugging like a train, and as he walked Raven could feel his sneaker bottoms crushing the row of crispy flowers planted beside the picket fence dividing Charles' yard from the neighbors'. The speckled mastiff, leashed to its post, was sleeping on the grass in the other yard and in neither of the houses were any lights on. Raven turned between two trees and under the sag of a blue hammock, and facing the back of Charles' house, which had one floor, he looked intently at the wooden shutters across each of the windows. Behind one pair of these shutters, Charles had his bedroom, and although Raven thought he remembered its location from a previous secret visit, he feared knocking on the wrong one and waking up Charles' sister or parents. Yet he had to do this, had to get Charles out of his bed and down to the residence, and calling him over the phone would have been the worst of his options, a sure way to unnerve his family.

"Qui est la?" came a voice, Charles' voice, after Raven had tapped on the wood several times. "Que est l' idiot?"

And Raven, in a whisper, identified himself, declaring that they had an emergency. He heard Charles grumbling and rising from his bed, and when Charles had released the shutters, pulling them inward from where they joined, he said they would have to change their plans. They would have to leave Martinique sooner than they had projected. Just a half hour ago Bianca Bishop had come to his room, and from this visit, sudden and startling, he had been forced to make the assumption that she had seen him following her. She must have seen him during those weeks when he had been doing his spying, and inside the residence she had probably wanted to frighten him off with tough brash language.

"But you were so careful," Charles said, pouchy-faced, still in a daze. "How could that happen?"

"Don't get nervous."

"Did she see her mother?"

"She saw her."

"And?"

"I had to decide. Let Bianca go out again or take her down right then."

"Don't tell me. You used the chloroform."

"I didn't need it," Raven said. "I hit her with something and tied her up with my bedsheets."

"Superbe."

"It's not so bad. She's in my room - gagged also - and I told her mother to watch her."

But could they trust Caroline? Could they rely on this woman? Raven recalled the drizzly night when she had appeared at the residence - the first unexpected visitor at his door - and he remembered how she had curtly said that she would help him kidnap Bianca. Crying, she had told him about her romance with Larry and she had described how his best friend, his lifelong friend, had been butchered by her husband. As for her husband, he thought she had flown to California where they had once lived, and Caroline insisted that she was primed to take Larry's place in the abduction scheme. To state the obvious, she wanted revenge against her husband, but she did not think that she should report him for Larry's murder. There had been her husband's threat to have her killed if she went to the police, but more important than that (she knew she could get police protection if she asked for it), was her desire to wreck him emotionally. By kidnapping Bianca, by extracting from Eric a six-figure ransom, by making him writhe with the valid worry that he might lose his beloved daughter, she would be digging into his heart, putting him through the hell he deserved.

"But you're her mother," Raven had said. "She's your daughter, too."

"She's all I have to use against him."

So much poison in her voice, so much sorrow in the greenness of her eyes, and Raven was convinced that she had loved Larry. But would her resolve in this thing last? Once they had Bianca Bishop on Charles' boat -if they ever got her onto the boat - would Caroline soften and crack? The loss of a love and the wish for vengeance had given Caroline a witch's malignity, but as the days went by and her daughter suffered, her hatred for Eric might be overridden by maternal instinct. 'Watch her,' Raven told himself. 'On the boat, always watch her.'

He and Charles were nose to nose at the window ledge, and the momentary closeness afforded him a magnified view of Charles' pock marks. These must have formed during his adolescence - miniscule craters in the dark skin - and just as unflattering for his face was the unusual length of his jaw, somehow a jaw that held his face in a perpetual cast of dejection. To offset this peculiarity, Charles wore a beard, a well-trimmed goatee, but that along with the fullness of his lips gave him the look of a satyr. As Raven had said to him, uglier men did exist in the world, but Charles had never been pleased with his face and even the present attention from Raven seemed to be a scrutiny he could not bear. He backed some way from the window ledge and looked up over Raven's head as if to see whether someone in the house next door was observing them. Or was he thinking of the neighbor's dog, the highly strung mastiff, which might awaken and start barking? That could be disastrous, to have Charles' parents and the people over there roused by the mindless animal, and so Raven tried to speak even lower than he just had. He asked Charles to get dressed, said they would have to carry Bianca out of his room and down to the boat before dawn. They had *The Lucky Blonde* stocked with everything they needed for their departure, and he saw nothing to keep them from setting sail by morning.

"It was supposed to be in a week," Charles said.

"I told you the schedule's changed."

"But this fast?"

"What's the problem? Bianca happened to come to us - lucky stroke - and all we have to do is get her out of the residence, into your car, and down to the pier. It shouldn't be hard at this hour. Use the chloroform."

Raven waited, expecting agreement, but Charles had become as rigid as a waxwork. He was a statue in blue underpants, and with his face turned to the sky he seemed to be consulting with higher powers, soliciting these powers for celestial guidance. In that position he looked tormented, harried by deep-seated pressures, and when he finally did break his paralysis and move from the window, he still had in him the heaviness of an afflicted person.

"I don't know now. I don't think I can."

"Charles..."

"How can I just leave her here?"

"By forcing yourself," Raven said. And despite the risk of

making noise, of disturbing Charles' parents or that mastiff, he leapfrogged over the window ledge and tugged Charles forward by the hand. Charles, as lax as a straw, did not resist him and he led Charles through the open door and into the grey darkness of the passage. There he had a choice - to go left or right - but from his earlier visit to the house he could recall that Charles' sister slept one door to the left. He dragged his arm against the wall until he felt the rusty latch, and in the room with the muslin-shaded lamp shining, with the stuffed pandas and the marble-eyed tigers, in this room where Danielle would sit and talk to her gallery of female dolls, he drew Charles over to the bed and ordered him to look down, to stare with clarity at Danielle, to consider the value of this girl who truly belonged in a mental hospital. After 19 years of life, a life governed by the tyranny of her dementia, only doctors would be able to help her, and he, Charles, had to do what was best for himself.

Charles nodded in accord but remained transfixed. From her neck to her feet, his sister lay covered by a pink blanket, and her hair, black and abundant, a forest of hair, hid a good portion of her face. Nevertheless, Raven could see her angelic cheeks with their unblemished honeylike color, and for all his impatience to depart from the house, he felt a pinch of sadness for Danielle, sadness for a girl with physical appeal but too much psychological confusion. Was she incurable? He knew from Charles that she was going through a depressed period and he knew as well that she had been in this pit of gloom since the night that she had discovered and destroyed the pornographic video collection her brother had kept on his boat. Regressive before, she had gone back still further since her explosion on his boat, and a proof of this was the lamp that she needed to have on beside her whenever she slept alone in the dark. She was just so vulnerable, so dependent on others for her survival, and even as Raven was thinking this, she rolled from her back onto her side and slipped one hand from beneath the blanket to put her thumb into her mouth.

"She won't wake up," Charles said. "We give her medication to sleep."

Raven could note the effect of this drug by the calm and rhythmical pattern of her breathing, by the deathly composure in her golden face, by the lack of any muscular tension in the arms and legs that had now pushed off the pink blanket. Exposed to the light in her shroud of a robe, she lay on her side in the middle of the mattress, lay with knees to chest in a fetal posture, and through some spark of intuition, a mental bridging that was like telepathy, Raven knew that within himself Charles had begun to debate the question of whether or not he should kill Danielle. Within himself, point by point, Charles was devising an argument for murder. But would this act, in the case of Danielle, even merit a word as guilt-provoking as murder? Where was the crime in killing Danielle if there was no crime in killing a horse racked by the pain of a broken leg? Like the horse that would never run, she was a cripple whose disability would be chronic, and left on her own in this house, stranded by herself with their sot of a father and their kind but dour mother, left to meet each endless day without the hope of seeing Charles, she would feel so lonely and desperate that she might lapse into catatonia. Her depression might lead to a status worse than death. Mercy then; Charles could wield the hand of mercy by lifting a pillow off the bed and pressing it down over her face, holding it there until she smothered, but Raven did not like the idea because of what the parents might do after they found Danielle in the morning. The father? The fat, bald hulk of a man who Charles likened in appearance to a frog? Who could determine what he would do beyond go stumbling with grief for his rum? But Charles' mother, always competent, would certainly notify the police. Through her tears she would give a statement, and once those men connected the death of the sister to the vanishing of the brother, once they linked his vanishing to the absence of his boat, once they did some elementary reasoning which might take five whole ticks of the clock, they would send out a radio alert annoucing Charles as the primary suspect, now missing, now gone to sea. Then would come the coastal unit searching for the boat by water and air, by cutter and helicopter, and before they, on *The Lucky Blonde*, ever got far from Martinique, they would be the objects of a hunt completely unrelated to their abduction of Bianca Bishop. It was clear: Charles had to leave his sister alive so that nobody would come looking for them.

"Think of the money," Raven said. "Think of the freedom you'll have on your own."

But did he need to repeat all this? Did he have to persuade Charles all over again? Charles had moved to the side of the bed towards which his sister was curled, and Raven watched him sit on the mattress with one leg hanging down to the floor and one bunched up against the rubbery blackness of his stomach. From the foot of the bed and with growing fascination, Raven watched him, and he began to feel the heat of voyeurism's pleasure when Charles reclined upon the bed, turned suddenly onto his hip and with one arm around her waist, flattened himself to his sister's body. She unconscious by the force of a drug and with her flesh that was the color of honey veiled only in the whitest of robes, he beginning to kiss her mouth and wearing just the blue underpants - to Raven this love of brother for sister might have been something distinctly erotic had he not been counting the minutes.

But soon enough the cocks would crow and the traffic would bring its noise and grit; soon enough their enemy the sun would blaze forth like an unwanted spotlight. Raven murmured through his teeth, shook the bed, cleared his throat with the most obvious artificiality, but still Charles kept his mouth to his sister's and still his arm encircled her waist. Now that arm had begun to slide, to uncoil and extend like a black snake, and as with one hand he played with her hair, the black wildness, so with his other he squeezed the buttocks that even through the white robe bulged with a sublime definition.

Fingers busy, tongue licking his sister's lips, eyes going from open to closed to open again, Charles was becoming a slave to the lust he had repressed in himself for years. Carried away on his crest of desire, he never once peeked a glance at Raven, and to Raven this seemed a voyeur's ideal. In his pants Raven felt the acute enlargement, the itching as from an assault of spiders, but despite this yearning to reach for his zipper and fondle himself, he knew quite well that he would have to speak with the voice of constraint. He had to get Charles back on the track that led to departure and so with this aim in his thoughts, he began to rehash the very advantages Charles himself had said he would have when he fled his home. Wherever he went, Raven reminded him, he would have no parents to support, no job selling cars, no neighbors so close and who knew him so well that he often felt as if he were living in a cage of glass. And guilt should have no part in his mind since he would be letting his parents keep the money he had saved from the car business. Was this not consideration? Through the boredom of his adult years had he not done everything he could for a sister with an illness and a father who drank? The ties holding a family together were also the ties that could strangle one's life, but in the future, if he so wished, he could mail his family a card saying he was fine and would never forget them.

"I'm coming," Charles said. "I just want to remember her body."

And so his hands travelled to her breasts, he lavished kisses on her neck and chin, he pressed his nose to the clumped black hair so that he could breathe in its scent. Despite an overall calm, a surprising sedateness, Charles had the moisture of tears in his eyes, and Raven himself felt sympathetic as he recollected the night he had cut his own connection to home. He remembered the night when he had married, when he had taken the wedding vows and then been obliged to kill his bride and her freakish clan of a family, and how in that mansion in upstate New York he, too, had gone through a ritual of touching and smelling a woman he loved in order to stamp into his being a permanent record of how she was shaped and how she smelled.

"We'll have Bianca," Raven said. "That'll be something to cheer you up."

Bianca the blonde, the blonde with the meaty thighs and the swimmer's shoulders, and Charles, of course, had his obsession with blonde-haired women. Almost every film in his collection of pornographic video cassettes had featured a blonde actress, platinum-blonde, dirty-blonde, strawberry blonde or a yellowish tint of blonde, and on his boat, out at sea, they would have Bianca defenseless, would have her bound inside a cabin. For himself, Raven thought, none of this was problematic, but what would Caroline do when she saw that Charles expected to have the use of her daughter? Would sexual use, Bianca's ravishment, be more than Caroline could stand? She as yet did not know that Charles had this obsession with blondes, and Raven could see himself jumping between them, having to stop them from ripping at each other's throats.

Beside the bed and next to the lamp, Charles was on his feet again, and he tenderly fixed his sister's nightdress. He pushed a lock of hair off Danielle's face and spread the pink blanket over her body. With this much done, he lifted his arms but kept looking down, engrossed perhaps by a reminiscence, and Raven had to poke him in the ribs to get him moving. Charles walked out like a zombie. In the hall it was Raven who shut the door, and in Charles' room, to expedite things, Raven helped Charles pack his clothes.

Chapter Thirteen

As tradition decreed she shared his last name, and on paper, in accordance with the document filed somewhere, she was still linked to him as his wife, but the woman sitting across from him with her hands on the table and the light of triumphant revenge in her face had become for Eric the object of a hate pure and cold. He could not imagine feeling a hate more consuming than this one. The blonde mound of hair that in a different epoch he had liked to lather himself, washing it for her from the side of the tub while she lay up to her neck in the water - this same hair he now wanted to burn, strand by strand, while she screamed. The genetic blessing of the high cheekbones, as balanced in form as any model's - these he wanted to break with a hammer. He wanted to see her milky skin turned into gashes and running blood; he would have felt no irresolution pulling out her fingernails with tongs. Barbarous thoughts? Sadistic imaginings? Quite, quite, and as a man dedicated to yoga, to the higher planes of spirituality, he was not proud to have these thoughts. But just as he knew that he had been justified in killing Caroline's recent lover (to punish her, at long last, for all her infidelities), so he knew that if ever a person deserved torture, then Caroline, his wife, was it.

A Saturday morning with the cobalt sun sending its warmth through the window glass, with the honks of geese and the quacks of ducks coming from the woods behind the house, and he had been doing his daily calisthenics with Ashok and the midget. He had been thinking of the toast and yogurt they would have for breakfast, and of the meditation they would start at noon. But then she had entered, disrupting everything; his wife had arrived using the key he should have taken from her when she'd left. They heard the door open and Caroline's voice, Caroline announcing herself in the hall, and when she came to the exercise room she set down a suitcase of black leather.

"Surprised to see me?"

He thought that her tan, a bronze iridiscence, had been acquired in California, but she said she had never gone to California. Nor had she meant it when she had told him she would go to California. She had flown instead to the Caribbean, Martinique, and there she had 'looked in on' their daughter. Looked in on Bianca? What did that mean? But Caroline only closed one eye and rubbed the tops of her fingers together, and Eric was put in mind of a witch licking her chops over evil machinations.

"You didn't," he said. "You didn't hurt Bianca?"

Caroline demanded that he talk to her one on one. She said he would have to listen to her without his mentors, Ashok and the midget, close by. Above all else, it was her arrogance, her poise, her tone of rock-hard certainty, that made him feel dread, and bowing to her will in this mood of dread, he grudgingly asked his mentors to leave. That they did, in their ragtag clothes and floppy sandals, but before they went they each gave him a coded glance making him aware that they stood ready to act, to help, to serve him exactly as they had done when he had erased that lover of Caroline's. "Fiends," said Caroline, stepping to the window, watching them walk to the part of the woods where they had their private shack. "Haven't you learned they're just living off you?"

Suitcase in hand, she zipped off toward the dining room. Eric looked at her white tennis sweater and the black pants cut to hug her waist. At arm's length, across from one another, they sat down, and here at this oakwood table where he, Caroline and Bianca had as a family eaten their meals together, she the enemy who was his wife blasted him with her trump card. "It's simpler than fighting you in court," she said, her laugh a taunt he would hear in his dreams, and to give him the proof that she was not lying she showed him a photograph of Bianca, roped by the wrists to the posts of a ship's bunk. In that bed she lay on her back with neither a gag nor a blindfold on, but up near the collar of her khaki blouse, a breast-revealing hole had been torn. And there was a third rope, orange-yellow against the blue of her jeans, keeping her ankles lashed together. Awful enough, this picture, and to maximize its impact, Caroline put a cassette machine before him, the button for playing already pressed.

"...they have me on a boat...they'll kill me if you don't pay.. they'll kill me..just drop me overboard in these ropes..please, please...just do what she says when she comes flying up there..do it no matter what you think of her...I can't tell you what it's like to be tied up..."

Bianca speaking with a parched voice, a trembly voice, yet

trying her best to sound courageous. Appalled, Eric stopped the machine. He ejected the tape. Any more of that voice in the next few seconds and he would be unable to contain himself looking at his wife's leer of triumph; the static anger held in his muscles would burst out into mortal violence.

From the thick of the woods he heard gunshots, rifle fire, and with these reports the ducks and geese inhabiting the ponds began to clamor madly. Ashok and the midget were hunting again despite the revulsion he had expressed over their bloodspilling hobby, and he did not want to let Caroline see that this demoralized him further.

"They still shoot birds and cook them?" she asked.

"Sometimes."

"What peaceful men of the spirit."

"Just tell me what it is you want. Your price."

She named it, the figure, and as he should have foreseen, it came as a crushing blow to his plans for buying the leafy island off Sri Lanka. He had his heart set on owning that island, on going with Ashok and the midget so that he could close himself off from the world and live exclusively for his meditations, like a monk. But the paying of the ransom would deplete his bank accounts, preclude the purchase. His net worth, his total value, was just over a million-and-a-half dollars; if he paid the ransom and then sold everything he had, including the house, he would not have the money to buy the island. But what could he do? Refuse to pay and let his only child die? Bianca had a mother who had become the true fiend here, who could sit by and see her own daughter trussed up, held prisoner, fed by others like a dog, and she had even left Bianca alone with the two guys she was abetting. Who could know what those animals had done, or were doing, to Bianca?

"You'll get her back," Caroline said. "All you have to do is follow my instructions perfectly."

She seemed to be growing in her chair, swelling with the confidence borne of having the upper hand, and Eric said that he should have killed her when he had disposed of her lover.

"Too late now," Caroline answered. "Now you have to follow my instructions. But I mean it. You're to do exactly as I say. No deviations, no tricks, or she dies."

She nodded for emphasis, and out in the woods - were Ashok and the midget slaughtering the birds? - the relentless gunfire continued.

*****

All afternoon, while Caroline made full use of the house, reading a magazine in the living room, cooking herself lunch in the kitchen, Eric sat at the desk in his study. He sat in misery adding numbers, checking his bank books, deciding from where he would draw the funds needed to keep Bianca alive. And Ashok and the midget, who had left the woods a blood-soaked mess filled with the corpses of geese and ducks, kept to themselves inside their cabin, since Caroline, when talking to Eric, had forbidden her husband from involving the pair in this transaction.

*****

"All I know is that we'll be flying from New York City," Eric said.

"Flying where?" asked Ashok.

"To the Caribbean."

"But to which island?"

"I don't know yet. She hasn't told me."

The moon above the trees shone with the luster of a minted penny, the woods still smelled of feathers and blood, some unowned dogs from the railroad yard of the nearest town had come to the area to feast on the litter of dead birds. In the house, after reading in bed, Caroline had gone to sleep, reclaiming her room like a wayward queen returned to her castle chamber for a night, and here in the cabin lit by a candle fixed in the mouth of a soda bottle, Ashok and the midget in their white dhotis sat lotus-like on their straw mats.

"When we get to the airport," Eric said. "That's when she'll tell me."

He was walking from wall to wall in the hut, taking eight strides, wooden as a robot, for each slow crossing of the hard dirt floor, and it seemed as if he could hear the dogs growling, chewing, feeding on the bones and meat in the woods. Ashok and the midget, stiff on their mats, looked like sculptures modeled from clay, but he could see their pupils moving as they watched him go through his pacing. They were, he thought, his surrogate family, his mentors and his confidants, but during this crisis they had also become a tribunal, a two-man court, and he himself was the one they were judging.

"Things couldn't be worse," he admitted. "Giving in like this to my wife. But I can't just let Bianca die."

Somewhere in the south on the waves of the sea was a

boat with his kidnapped daughter on it, and what was the island in the Indian Ocean compared to the ropes around her wrists, the ropes around her ankles, that rip near the collar of her khaki shirt? How important was his dream of blessed isolation when he thought of the pleading and the fright he had heard coming from Bianca's voice on the tape? Yet Ashok and the midget shared his dream of buying the island and going there to live, of living on the island and forgetting the world, and the payment of the ransom would dash their hopes as much as it would dash his. Perhaps this explained their call for daring, for the risk of trying to save Bianca without turning over the money, and Eric had to tell them once more that he did not know where the exchange for Bianca would happen. All he knew is that it would happen in the Caribbean, that he would have to tote a satchel with the money and fly to the tropics with his wife. He had already disobeyed his wife merely by discussing the abduction with them, and to involve them actively, as in a rescue attempt, if such an attempt were even feasible, might result in Bianca's death.

"No," he said, and again, "No." He would not allow them to do anything that might endanger Bianca's life. But Ashok and the midget were inflexible, two judges declaring him guilty of cowardice, and as he kept pacing through the hut with his disjointed lumbering steps, the pair insisted that he take the chance, let them see if they could carry off a rescue mission.

"Why did you tell us at all?" said Ashok. "You could have said nothing and gone with your wife, paid the money, and told us afterwards. Isn't it because you want to try something?"

"No," Eric said, refusing to yield. "It's not." But then an idea came to his mind, and Eric tripped to a dead stop. He did not know where his wife was holding their airplane tickets, but he did know the date on which they were flying and he also knew that a limited number of airline companies flew from New York City to the Caribbean. If he phoned each of these airlines to inquire about all Caribbean flights on that day, and if with his credit cards he booked two reservations on each flight, he might be able to get his mentors onto the same plane as him and Caroline. Ashok and the midget could shadow them to the airport by car, see which plane they were taking, and then use the correct reservations to board that plane. All of them might fly to the south, and to ensure that his mentors would have two seats far from the seat his wife would have, he would reserve on each airline two places in the section for non-smokers. Caroline, as he had noticed that afternoon, still went through pack after pack of filtered cigarettes.

"It'd be a gamble," he said to the pair after he had disclosed the idea. "She might see you on the plane."

But he quickly conceded that the risk was worth it: during the exchange for his daughter, Ashok and the midget might have the opportunity to intervene, to ambush the other two abductors. The midget had the body honed like a gymnast, had the hands and feet that were murderous weapons when he struck his karate blows, and despite a paunch with the softness of a pudding, Ashok could acquit himself fighting, too. Weeks ago, when he had done away with Caroline's lover, they had shown their battle capabilities, and he knew from their hunting of the woodland fowl that they themselves had the nerves for killing.

"We'll do it," he said. "And for Bianca's sake, we'll pray that it works."

He ran through the woods smelling the odor of the dead birds not yet eaten by the scavenging dogs, and for the rest of the night, while Caroline slept on in her room, he made the phone calls from the desk in his study.

Chapter Fourteen

Sometime after Guadeloupe, after their stop at the port and her mother's departure, it had begun. The two guys, Charles and Raven, had been keeping themselves in check until then, but sometime after her mother had left the boat they'd started to do more than just look at her body. With her mother on the boat she had still been a captive, her wrists worn red from the bite of the ropes, her cell of confinement the sultry cabin, yet neither of the men had become physical in the way that she most feared. Her mother was an enemy, the scourge of her life, but while on the yacht with these two deviants, her mother had also been her protector.

"We took her for the money, Charles. Not for anything else."

Her mother had said that before getting off, before leaving them at the Guadeloupe port, but none of this made any difference right now because she felt as if she were dying. Like a leak from a faucet, the blood kept trickling from between her thighs, and she did not see how she would last until her mother came back with the money.

And if he doesn't pay? If he lets me die? What if his gurus have brainwashed him and they tell him to forget all about me?

Once she had lived like the other people, the people who associated home with love, and once she had been fragile. She could remember that former self, that past incarnation, and with the despairing laugh of the wounded, the imprisoned, the person closing in on death, she remembered how bothersome it had seemed just to take out the garbage when it rained. Born into wealth and a world of trimmings, of fine art and Persian carpets, she had gone through her indolent life as if its comforts were her birthright, and even during the months in Martinique, during that span of voluntary exile, she had been nourished by the thought of what would be awaiting her when she went home. There for entertainment she had television and the box of discs for her CD player, and whenever she wanted to go somewhere she had her speedy Italian roadster. But was all of that real? Would she find everything where it had been if she did return from the boat? Now her house and the things she owned seemed like pictures invented by a dream, and her world had become this stifling cabin where she had to beg for a drink of water.

Fighting off panic, she asked herself what she could do. Neither of the ropes around her wrists had lost any of their tension, the two bedposts to which she was tied had the unbreakable strength of brass, in her stomach the enzymes were clashing because she needed to have food. This was suffering, concentrated pain, and she could smell her uterine blood as it ran between her thighs and onto the towel laid across the bunk. It appeared there could be no surviving this, no hope of dramatic escape, and with the cabin itself so black - the porthole was closed, the cabin light out - she began to have a vision of herself dead and discarded in the water, dead yet with open eyes, a corpse that would be floating with the current until its bleeding attracted the sharks.

Think. Think. Can't I do anything?

From her very first moments on the boat, when she had understood that she was a hostage, she had been lying in fear of the American because of those weeks when he had followed her through the streets of Fort de France. She had thought that he was a guy obsessed with the wish to invade her body, to use her body however he pleased, but after her mother had left the yacht to take the ransom demand to her father, it had been Charles who slavered like a brute, who kept staring her up and down with his pock-marked goatish face. At liberty to act, he'd licked her on the mouth and he had talked gibberish about her hair, the blondeness of it, as if that alone is what excited him.

"I remember this blonde I was with in Miami. We did it on the beach in the middle of the night."

To get at her, to spread her legs, Charles had removed the piece of rope binding her ankles. But he had done nothing to free her wrists and so she had known that struggling against him would be useless. She told herself to put her mind at a great distance from her body, to think of the sunsets, orange as fire, that she had watched when she was a child living near the shore in southern California; but she could not achieve this disengagement with the nausea in her rising. Pinned beneath him and feeling his weight, she had to suck hard to draw in air, and on his breath as it hit her face she could smell the cheese from his lunch. He mauled her breasts with his fumbling hands and then ordered her to ask for his sex, but even when he had her where he must have wanted, had her unclothed from the waist down, he cursed at her for showing no joy and insisted that she blubber and moan. "Say that you love it," she heard him whisper, and from these demands for ecstatic crooning, she could guess that on Martinique he had been addicted to pornographic films. Only in those, with their distortions, with their images coming from the fever of male fantasy, could a woman who was being raped turn into a nymphomaniac.

She spoke the words he told her to speak, she made the sounds he told her to make, she bit her lip and fought with herself to keep her tears from spilling into view. 'This isn't me,' kept running through her head. 'This isn't happening to me,' and finally she could feel a split in herself as if her mind refused to accept what her body had to endure. Looking straight up at the low white ceiling, she began to examine the shadows there, a spidery pattern of intersecting lines, and among them she saw a blue-winged fly that did not move for several minutes. Arresting, fascinating, each of these details, and though she was forced to continue with her orgiastic noises, she found herself able to effect a modified self-hypnosis, a mental deadening that helped her go numb.

How many times over how many days had Charles come walking into the cabin while unbuckling the flap in his pants? Against her face as he pressed down on her she would feel his thistly beard, and from his breath would blow that odor of the food he had last eaten: fish or cheese or onions or peppers. Mostly he would come when the sun was up, the light shining hotly through the porthole, and often in the circle of that hole she would see, black and glinting, the frosty eyes of the American, a voyeur with his own peepshow.

Please, father. Don't let me die here.

In the trashy novels that she had read to ease her boredom in Martinique, the heroine who was abused by the villain would always find safety in the arms of the hero. You would know as you read those books how the story would resolve; you, the reader, could rest assured that the hero would brave all tricks and dangers until he rescued the woman he loved. But would her father be that resolute? He had as advisors the Indian men to whom she as his daughter was nothing, and to pay a big ransom to her mother, his dire enemy, might be too humiliating for him. There was no predicting what he would do, and moreover she had the wound inside, the slow but continual bleeding, the thought that she might die of the blood loss before her mother ever returned. Somehow or other she would have to save herself, get to land, and her attempt at escape would have to be soon, while she still had the strength in her to move.

It was night. The coolness of the pitch-black cabin told her that, and from the quiet on board the yacht, she presumed that both her abductors had gone to sleep in the other cabin. She could hear the chain for the anchor clinking whenever the boat swayed at all, and the sound of waves, tumultuous breakers, let her know as it had through the evening that they had dropped the anchor near land. A shoreline was close and maybe people, too; though here in the tropics land could mean a stump of rock with a coconut tree. If she took the risk, did it now, and through some luck got off the boat, she would be swimming for dear life toward an island that could be anything.

"Hey," she said, giving her voice the ring of impatience. "I have to use the bathroom please."

No answer came, nothing whatsoever, and she was compelled to shout her appeal until she heard them talking drowsily.

"You want to go?"

"I went the last time."

"Are you sure?"

"Hold on. I think it is better if I do it."

The American then, and she waited for him to insert the key, release the padlock, open up the cabin door. Light from the passage entered with him, flooded the cabin, and after the expected seconds of blindness she saw him above her looking down, his eyes much softer than she had remembered them.

"Does it really hurt?"

"I've had to go for an hour."

"I meant the bleeding. Can I give you anything to make it hurt less?"

Around her she had the clean white walls of the cabin, under her thighs the white towel was an absorbent for the trickle of blood, and now with the door to the cabin open, she could better hear the crash of the surf as it broke upon that shoreline. In the other cabin, across the passage, Charles had begun to whistle something, a catchy Martinican song, but here with her the American guy seemed to have none of this buoyancy, clapping one hand over his forehead.

"I'm only asking because - I don't know - maybe I can get

130

something for you."

"You could let me go."

"Something to help you sleep perhaps."

"You could let me go somewhere."

"If we could only stop the bleeding."

Violation had been one thing, one type of horror, and with the American it was the feeling of having the black eyes canvass her as if she were just damaged goods. Above her waist she still had on the khaki blouse that Charles had torn, but since the removal of her pants and drawers, neither the American nor his friend had brought anything as a cover for her legs. Thus exposed, and still lashed to the bed, she could but look at the American as he carried on his inspection, and she had to refrain from kicking at him when he knelt by the bunk with his hands on her knees and spread her legs quite wide.

"Charles, I think you've killed her."

"She won't die."

"She will if we can't stop the bleeding."

And this, Raven's indictment, started them quarrelling, though even while he and Charles were yelling, the American kept his hands on her knees and his face above her pelvis, never taking his angry eyes off the dripping zone of her wound.

"You may have wrecked everything," Raven said. "We may not get the money now."

"What? Her mother will turn on us?"

"It's possible."

"Mais, non! She isn't a mother to begin with."

"That's not the point. You went too far and Caroline explicitly said don't hurt her."

"You didn't complain while you were watching."

She listened to Charles defending his actions, shouting from the darkness of the other cabin, and she heard him say she had been his due after the sacrifice he had made in deserting his weak, lonely, suffering sister.

"Please," she said, cutting in when he stopped. "I really have to get to the bathroom."

Only during the times when she asked to use the toilet would they untie the ropes on her wrists (meals came to her on a fork or spoon held by either one of her captors), and Raven hurriedly did this now while she lay as dead as a doll and looked at him with droop-lidded eyes. If she could convince him through her appearance that she was almost gone, with little of her strength and no will left, he would have to lower his guard.

First one wrist slipped free, her left, and then her right wrist fell loose, and as she laid them across her chest observing the bands of discoloration, Raven told her to swing off the bunk, walk in front of him, keep her arms hanging down so that he could see them. She felt no pain when she got up, a surprising development, but with the wobbling that she gave to her knees she let him think that she was on the verge of passing out. "I'm sorry for all this," he said, not without a trace of melancholy, and she was nearly over at the cabin door when to reassume a firmer control he grabbed her by the back of the neck. "Slow now," he said. "Go slow." But she had stopped her forward motion, beginning to spin despite his grasp, and with a speed that was stoked by her fear, she slapped at his hand with her left arm and kicked her knee up against his groin. His mouth opened mutely, like a person doing mime, his eyes lost focus as they went wet, and for that moment of a heartbeat's duration, she had him before her unmanned and defenseless, had right there a glorious picture of this voyeur's immobilizing pain. Then she had to continue, strike him again, and she drove her head into his mouth as if she were a horned ram. Through her hair and against her scalp she could feel the edge of a tooth, sharp enough to prick her skin, but she knew how effective her butt had been when pulling back from him she saw the slit in his lips and the splotch of blood.

She retreated through the door, turned up the passage, sprang for the three metal steps leading to another door and the deck. The sky looked starless, presaging a storm, and as she ran across the deck she heard again the thunder of the waves hitting the coast of that island. "Don't let her get into the water..Fucking hell." Both were coming, pounding after her, but she had a hold on the deck's railing and her feet going over the highest bar. A final push and off she went, out into space, and she tried her best to arch her body and so prevent a belly flop dive.

Would they pursue? Could they swim? She sliced through the water thinking this, descended through the silence of the blackness wishing that she could swim to the shore underwater, and as she began her ascent for air, she heard the plops of the splashes made by her abductors jumping in. With a fire in her nose and an ache in her lungs she came up to the surface coughing, and she started treading water with her legs while wiping at the hair over her eyes. Ahead, she saw, were the white-crested swells rolling in their natural course toward land; behind, it followed, must be the boat. She twisted round to face the boat and scan the extent of water she had covered, and up nearby in that gap rose the heads of Charles and Raven, heaving in the surf like oversized corks.

"You're going to drown," yelled Raven. "You won't get anywhere in that condition."

But it was he and Charles who were laboring, stirring up foam as they fought with the water, and this gave her the confidence to think that she could outswim them both. Nearly every day while in Martinique she had gone swimming for the exercise, and though her body had been hurt, she still felt that she could make it do what she wanted.

She dunked her head and changed direction. As she returned to the surface she went into her crawl. She had landed in the water feeling a slap of sudden coldness, but now that was past and the water felt warm and she had gotten her second wind. Her wound alone caused discomfort, abdominal pain that would build and ebb, burn and cease, and whether her pursuers were gaining or not she did not care to know about so long as she did not feel their hands locking onto her arms and legs, trying to pull her back through the water and over to the yacht.

The crest of a wave lifted her high, carried her forward, and passed on through her toward its breaking point. She knew she was getting close to the shore, into the area of roughest surf, and for these reasons she began to swim faster. But while turning her head for one of her breaths, she mistimed the action and swallowed some water, and the coughing that resulted upset her rhythm, so that all at once she was flipping underwater as a breaking wave hit her from behind. The sea became whiteness and crashing sound, spray and bubbles and elemental force, but she knew better than to put up a fight and in the funnel of powerful current held her breath while flopping about.

When the maelstrom slowed, she was floating on her stomach, and she felt herself pulled up and back. Seizing her chance to breathe again, she raised her head above the surface, but just as soon as she had inhaled, another wave came washing down. Again she was thrown, buffeted about, the vortex a rage of noise in her ears, and from somewhere along the unseen bottom grit swirled up into her face. Though scratched and dazed, she hung on calmly, and when the wave had receded she resurfaced. She discovered she could stand on the tips of her toes. Without her knowing it, the push of the waves had brought her even closer to the island, and in her sights she had a lava-black beach.

"I've got you..I've got you... For Christ's sake, don't choke me.."

The voice belonged to Raven, a yelling Raven, a Raven she could hear above the roar of the approaching whitecaps, and she looked back toward the deeper water. Everything there was a dark fuzziness, but it did seem from what she saw that Raven and Charles were wrestling. They were like beasts gone amok, their savagery turned against each other in a convulsive combat, and while they rolled and splashed and floundered, Raven never stopped his screaming.

"Grab my shoulders..my shoulders, Charles. If you can do that I can get you to the boat..."

They went into a clinch, chest to chest, but after these words a whole new meaning lay over the scene. Charles was drowning, going under, and Raven was attempting to rescue him.

"Who won't make it?" she shouted at Raven. "Who won't get anywhere?"

She dove beneath the surface and made the transition again to her crawl. In the shallows she stood, the water at her knees, and on legs that were cramping, bunching into knots, she walked up onto the beach. The cool black sand below, the euphoria of having solid earth, terra firma, under her feet, and she looked out to sea to continue watching Charles and Raven. But she had seen only one, and that Raven, when a wave rose up between them and the shore, a wave that gathered and filled her view. As it broke, dispersing its foam, she tried to spot the Martinican, but it was still Raven by himself and now he too sank under the water. Very soon, however, he had come up, and he began swimming toward the ghost-white yacht, paddling on his side as if too weary to bring his arms over his head.

Alive, she thought. She was hurt and bleeding, yet alive, and on this island, near this beach, there had to be someone who could help, who could give her clothes and get her to a doctor.

Chapter Fifteen

Past the southernmost town on the map, a fisherman's village with a cove full of dories, the asphalt ended and the road became dirt. It went by some ruins, gray rubble, that might have been a slave-era prison, and on a flat beyond the debris stood four white walls encompassing the shrines and tombs of a cemetery. More and more the road was curving, looping, doubling back on itself in the thickening brush, and to Eric, driving the rental car, there seemed to be no end to the rocks and holes. As he bucked in his seat he had to keep changing the slipping gearshift, and when the road began to climb, he started to doubt the car would make it, feared that with its groan of an engine it would conk out and not turn over so that he and Caroline would have to go the rest of the distance on foot, would have to walk for miles and miles to reach the place where she had promised the return of his daughter.

Last night it had rained, with cracks of lightning, but no heaviness had been purged from the air. He'd felt this at dawn when he awoke, and while dressing in the hotel he had wondered how a storm might affect the rendezvous, how a squall or choppy sea might compel the men on the yacht to hold Bianca longer than planned. Where were they exactly? Did they have their boat anchored offshore at the meeting spot? Up in the capital, at the hotel, Caroline had told him to get in the car and drive, to drive where she said and ask no questions, and he did not know how the abductors intended to work the exchange.

The land was forest by now, and green as jade. Eric assumed that they would be with the kidnappers soon. But the motor still had its irregular sound as if at any minute it would stall, and the stick for the gears kept refusing to hold. Through the windows he could feel electrical pressure, the pulsing calm that comes before rain, and in the road with its slosh and puddles, there had appeared red-orange crabs that were clumped several deep. Linked claw to claw, snagged on one another, they scrambled for their lives as the car moved ahead, and it must have been the sight of their sideways running that made Caroline laugh as she watched.

135

She was wife yet stranger, wife yet foe, a hated person sitting beside him in the passenger seat. On her lap she held the satchel that had gotten through customs here; the grouchy man at the airport inspection had discovered neither the false bottom nor the money packed beneath it. "Thanks," she had said when the man waved them on, and this morning, in her blue tennis shirt and white shorts, she could have been mistaken for a sightseeing tourist out for a spin through the rain forest. There on top of her blonde coif she had set her sunglasses, and in her hands she had a sandwich of ham and cheese on French bread. Hungry himself, Eric could smell the oil and vinegar and even the garlic in this sandwich, but what drove him up the wall was the hedonism in her eating, the way she had of chewing every morsel slowly, swallowing slowly, and then licking off her oily fingers. How, at a time like this, could Caroline eat, and eat no less like an epicurean?

"Enjoying yourself?" he asked.

"Not bad."

"So finish the goddamned thing already."

"I bought a sandwich for you, too."

"That was considerate. I don't want it."

But like a mother with a headstrong child, Caroline ignored his refusal and she pulled his sandwich from a paperbag lying across the brown satchel. Eric warded off her arm as if in that hand she held a knife, and because he had his attention on her, did not turn the steering wheel when something black flew past in the road. He felt the bump and heard the cry of a dog in pain, saw through the windshield as they kept going that it was a dog lean as a skeleton. After pressing the brakes, he decided not to stop, and in his mirror he watched it giving chase. It seemed to think the car was an animal that it could catch and hurt back, and apart from the limp it had as it ran, it looked unaffected by the glancing collision, unhampered in its speed.

"On these islands," Eric said, "there are too many wild dogs."

"Starving dogs," Caroline answered, and through the window on her side she hurled the sandwich he had refused. With her head out the window she called to the dog, invited it to eat what she had thrown, and as if it was her old pet, a dog familiar with her commands, it cut across the road on a diagonal and stopped by the bread and meat in the dirt. It had only wanted food, Caroline said, and equated human beings driving through the forest with delectable handouts.

The road snaked, the road plunged, the road meandered on. And the density of color, the brilliance of the reds and greens and purples, started to become too much for Eric. He felt menaced by the forest itself. Those tentacular branches to the left, that creeping plant over there - anything alive might reach from its tree and try to strangle him as he drove; in this forest, travelled though it was, he felt like a man encroaching on a place inhabited by hostile spirits. It seemed as if here, in such a surrounding, no human action could end very well, and he could but hope that the presence of an ally, the boldness of the midget, would help him do what he needed to do.

Fit for concealment, his size an advantage, the midget lay in the trunk of the car. Like invisible shadows, Ashok and the midget had made the plane trip without being seen by Caroline, and after landing in the capital, they had checked into a three-floor hotel across from the one he and Caroline took. With those two near, near and watching, Eric had begun to feel as if he could salvage the situation, could rescue his daughter and keep the ransom, and it had been this morning, outside the hotel, before Caroline stepped from her room, that he had put the limber midget into the car's trunk. Ashok, they had agreed, would have to wait in town, but for the rescue they wanted to mount, for their meeting with the abductors, the midget was the one with the necessary talents; he, not chubby Ashok, had a bobcat's swiftness and the lethal karate skills.

Behind the car, like a nagging ghost, the spindly black dog had reappeared. Despite its pause to eat and the bends in the road, the feral mutt had caught up with them, and Eric surmised that it wanted more food, expected them to throw another gift. But they had nothing left to give because Caroline had finished her ham and cheese sandwich, and besides that, not even she had any more interest in this dog's hunger. As she stared through the windshield, her chin to the dashboard, she pointed to a boulder white as chalk, and just beyond this she gestured to a track leading off toward the coast. Eric followed it. He could smell sea water and rot-choked swamp, and along with the sound of the dying engine he could hear waves and whispering surf. They had made it then, the car had held up, and when they came to the end of land, a black shingle, he saw in the water straight ahead the badly tilted body of a yacht.

"Is that it?" he said. *"The Lucky Blonde?"*

Scott Adlerberg

"That's the boat," Caroline answered.

But tilted? Slanted so much in windless air and on a smooth patch of sea? Neither his daughter nor the two men could be anywhere on this yacht, and Eric looked over the entire beach as if on its sand he would find their corpses.

"Where are they?" he asked. "What's going on?"

In the center of his bones, the very marrow, he felt a chill, and he began to feel even colder when he turned in his seat toward Caroline. Her expression had become so vacuous, so impenetrable, that Eric knew she had made the face to hide her own incomprehension.

"The boat looks abandoned, doesn't it?"

She gave him a reply he could not hear and reached for the handle on her door. Would she start running away with the satchel? The paleness in her face proved to Eric that she had been anticipating something different, something other than a derelict boat and a beach that was empty, and before she had walked three steps on the sand, Eric opened the driver's door thinking he would let the midget out. But Caroline was not running anywhere yet (and where in the forest, with its mud and swamp, could she run?); Caroline had come back to the car to rest one arm against the roof and stare at the leaning, drifting yacht.

The humid deadness in the air, the sky gray with low-lying clouds, the sea as clear as blue glass and sliding ashore in gentle waves - with all of this Eric imagined that he had arrived at the earth's edge, a final border, where everything existed in an unreal calm. By comparison, the dog, the unshakeable mutt, seemed frenetic in this stillness, coming to the beach and running along it, burrowing through some weeds nearby. Caroline kept on looking at the boat as if she was trying to will her partners into being, and her patent dismay at their non-appearance made Eric feel that now he had the upper hand, had the leverage to give the orders. But what had happened to Bianca? With this reversal of positions, Eric knew that he could grab the bag of money and tell the midget to knock off Caroline, but none of this would bring him any closer to finding Bianca and getting her home to safety.

"The dog's got something. You smell that?"

Caroline had said it, wrinkling her nose as she spoke, and Eric, too, smelled the stench of death. It came with the odors of the noxious plants growing from the muck where the dog was

138

probing, and as the dog backed through the weeds and on toward the black sand of the beach, Eric saw that in its mouth it was dragging a human leg. The leg was connected to a mud-covered body and when the dog got out of the ooze and onto the solid footing of the sand, it started to eat the prize it had found, biting into one of the thighs. And now Eric, forgetting Caroline, was sprinting across the beach to look, feeling the heat of nausea in his head, and he wanted to deny the body's nudity. He wanted to undo that coat of mud and the ghoulishness of the white lips stretched into a silent shriek. Bianca, his darling Bianca, his precious; and the open eyes in the puffy face seemed to be accusing him of a crime, blaming him for her death. Shot through with the blood of burst capillaries, her eyes yet retained a haunting focus, and they were saying from the world of the dead that he could have been a better father, that he could have been more involved in her life, that in recent months, absorbed with his yoga, he had become a distant man sending to her in Martinique nothing except the monthly check. Because of him, the eyes were saying, she had met her death on this beach.

Eric fell, groveled in the sand, began to weep. From behind him at the car he heard a door slam and he thought of Caroline jumping in the car to drive herself and the money away. He stood up to run, to prevent her from going, but then he remembered that he had taken the keys from the wheel. They were in his right hand, two keys on a ring, and he had pulled them from the ignition to unlock the trunk and let out the midget.

As Caroline watched from the driver's seat, the redness of anger in her face, Eric walked straight over to the trunk. He put the key in the slot and lifted the door, and after that things happened fast, with the midget hopping down to the ground, listening to Eric's set of instructions, running in his shorts and sleeveless shirt after the fleeing Caroline. Like a desperate fugitive, she had leapt from the car holding the satchel by its grip, and she ran across the sand towards the weeds and brush as if in there she had a hideout. However, she did seem to comprehend that she had nowhere to go, and in a flash Eric realized that she was not running to escape with the ransom; she just wanted to deprive him of having the money back. From near Bianca's body, which the dog was still eating, she threw the satchel into the mud and mire, and Eric felt sure that it would be gone forever, lost in some gummy pool.

"Kill her," he yelled, dashing across the beach himself. "No..wait..cripple her."

She made an effort to defend herself, but the midget's karate was overwhelming. Blow after blow from hand and foot hit her arms and her legs, and when she had fallen, helpless in the sand, the midget stopped and Eric came up.

"You'll die slowly," Eric said. "The sun will come out and you'll get hotter and hotter and hotter."

Her tears were flowing, as he wished, but through a titanic application of will, she gave him a hateful smile. And nothing he had said lessened his misery, nothing the midget had done to her brought a sense of revenge attained. All that money had sunk into mud no more easy to cross than quicksand, the black dog starved for a meal was stripping the flesh off his daughter, and he had not the foggiest notion of what had become of the two men who had held Bianca captive.

"It's over," he said. "Everything's over."

Ashok would be waiting in town, would ask to know what had happened, and he would have to tell his spiritual mentor that he no longer had the wealth to buy the little island in the Indian Ocean. Would that prompt Ashok and the midget to desert him? Would they leave him on his own and attach themselves to somebody richer? He needed Ashok and the midget now, and if they departed, his life would be a vacuum.

"Let's get going," he said. "I can't stand it here anymore."

The midget had established to his own satisfaction that the bag of money was lost, irretrievable, and as he turned from the weeds and swamp he kicked Caroline one last time. This elicited fresh tears, but again she showed them the defiant venomous smile.

"How do you think she died?" asked the midget.

"I don't know," Eric said.

"You think she drowned? Got washed up onto the beach? Maybe she escaped from the men but got caught somehow in the mud."

"It doesn't matter anymore," Eric said.

Bone and gristle, blood and muscle. Nothing else remained of Bianca's body after the dog's feeding frenzy, and Eric decided not to try bringing it back for cremation or burial. Nature had his daughter, nature in the form of the black dog, and the best he could do, though it would change nothing, was to have something built in her honor. He could do it at home, behind his

house, and every day he would go to the monument.
Every day, come sun or storm, he would put a flower there.

Scott *Adlerberg*

Epilogue

I don't know the exact location of this island. I can't even remember how long I was in the rubber motorboat after I got away from the yacht. *The Lucky Blonde?* Lucky for whom? Not for me, that's obvious, and not for Charles either. The guy couldn't even swim very well, and he had been living in Martinique almost his entire life. How can a person from an island, a tropical island, not have learned to swim well? He has all that water around, but he's like a man from a big city who has trouble enough floating in a pool. It's funny, when you think about it, but nothing was funny about Charles drowning. He went under, and Bianca, naked and bleeding, swam through the waves like a fish, and our whole plan died on the spot.

Everything collapsed right there, and all I could do was swim back to the boat and lie on the deck exhausted. Bianca did swim to an isolated beach, a beach in the forest, but there's no saying that she didn't find the forest road. That path from the beach goes to the road and I would have to bet that she did find it. Even hurt and naked she could have done that, walking for miles in one direction, pushing herself till a car came along or until she reached somebody's house. Then, I would guess, she told the cops, and she must have had her mother picked up as soon as Caroline landed at the airport with Eric Bishop and the ransom money.

So I had to take off. I couldn't let myself get caught. Everything in our plan had come to nothing, but I had the motorboat there to use and the yacht's stock of food. Let the police search for me. Let them comb the island and examine *The Lucky Blonde*. I've been on the run from police before and I would rather be dead than in prison.

Although, to be honest, I could consider this island a prison. The motorboat has become deflated - it must have had a small hole somewhere - and I haven't found anything else that I could use to leave here. It is a term of confinement that I have begun, and a thorough check of the place has told me that I am serving my time alone, that I am a prisoner living in solitary. I only wish I could determine where precisely this island is.

The weather is hot, the water off the island's shore is turquoise, the sky when sunny has a blueness so deep the color in the air seems palpable. The Caribbean still? It has to be, even though I can't remember how long I was in the rubber motorboat after I left *The Lucky Blonde*. I sat at the tiller controlling the boat and I know I became dizzy from the sun, but the rest of that trip is a blank in my mind, like something I dreamt but then forgot. However it happened, I ended up here, and I gradually adapted myself to the island. It has palm trees and bush, caves and a lake, and for eating I have its wild fruits and the crabs I catch on the beaches. I can survive here. I think I can last, but over time I might go crazy from the solitude.

Yes, my solitude is the real hardship, and this is the reason I often visit the island's cemetery. Green and shady, rimmed by four white walls, the cemetery is where I go when I want to rest in the afternoons, and to pass the hours I usually talk there to the dead. On one tombstone the name of Larry is inscribed, near that stands a slab dedicated to Charles, and Lisa has a plot marked by a tablet; Lisa the girl I loved and married, loved and killed.

I still don't think I made a mistake leaving her family the way I did, destroying those monsters I would have had to serve, and if I helped wreck Charles' family and also ruptured Bianca Bishop's, I can say in my defense that I did nothing out of meanness. My only objective was to further our plan. But who needs a family? I don't have one. I don't have anyone and here I am, still alive. By knowing the island and living on the barest essentials, I will endure this solitude for as long as it goes on, and I will not allow myself to crack up even if it is just me and the trees, me and the water, me and the graves of dear friends, the saddened dead.